# THE JUSTICE OF MARTIN BRAND

By
RAYMOND A. PALMER

ARMCHAIR FICTION
PO Box 4369, Medford, Oregon 97504

*For more information about Armchair Books and products, visit our
website at…*

**www.armchairfiction.com**

*Or email us at…*

**armchairfiction@yahoo.com**

# *INTERPLANETARY WAR WITH EARTH AS THE PRIZE!*

The half-crazed Martin Brand, who listened to classical music while rocketing toward a half-dozen enemy ships—atomic cannons blasting—was Earth's only hope.  The much embittered former spy for the Interplanetary Patrol was the only one who knew about the Martian spaceships that lay waiting in a hidden cavern on the Moon. But to warn Earth, Brand needed to forsake vengeance on the man who betrayed him and cost him everything he held dear.  Then there were the women: one who had sworn to kill him and another who had sworn to arrest him dead or alive. And if he made it that far, he'd have to fight his way to the surface through ten thousand Martians.   But that's why they called him "Suicide" Martin Brand. And even if he did succeed in warning Earth, war would flare across three worlds!

FOR A SECOND COMPLETE NOVEL, TURN TO PAGE 139

# CAST OF CHARACTERS

## MARTIN BRAND

*Jilted at the altar, he found solace in risky covert missions that usually pitted him against the worst humanity had to offer.*

## KATHLEEN DENNIS

*She had loved Martin Brand from afar for most of her life. Now it was her job to arrest him for murder!*

## JEFFREY KILLIAN

*This would-be conqueror spent a lot of time gloating over his past successes and had malicious plans set for Earth.*

## COMMANDER WILSON

*He knew something was very wrong on Luna—and he had to do something a little radical in order to prove it.*

## HAL ORSON

*He had to find out when and where the first alien strike was to take place. If he didn't, it could well spell doom for Earth!*

## ESTELLE CARTER

*This beauty planned a long time to gain her revenge. Oh…and also to rule the Earth. Too bad she was totally insane.*

# CHAPTER ONE

*Martin Brand was executed as a traitor and his coffin was enshrined in memory of a hero. Then a woman in love did a strange thing—she opened the coffin...and war flared across three worlds.*

"IT'S A crazy thing, Kathleen," Hal Orson said in a savage whisper. "Worse still, it can only hurt you. He's dead...why open up old wounds? You'll break your heart."

"It's already broken," Kathleen Dennis said in a tight, strained voice. "It broke the day they took him away, condemned as a traitor, and I believed it...until you told me the truth."

Orson stopped in the darkness and grasped her arm. "Kathy, please don't do it. You don't know how much trouble you can get into if you are caught at this mad scheme. You couldn't possibly explain why you did it—" Orson pulled her around until she faced him in the gloom of the tomb's interior. "Just why are you doing it?" he insisted. "Why! For the life of me I can't understand..."

"Why did *you* agree to come along in the first place?" she whispered fiercely.

He tried to see her face in the gloom, but it was only a pale oval, and for an instant he thought he saw something glistening, as though there were tears on her cheeks reflecting little glints of light from some unseen source. He lifted one hand and brushed his fingers across her velvet skin. They came away wet. He shook his head in irritation.

"Because I was his best friend—or as good a friend as he'd let anybody be. And because..." He fumbled for words, but the wetness on his fingers strangled them in his throat. To say more would only hurt her worse...

"Because you felt there was a possibility that I might be right," she finished for him; "That he might not be…"

"Kathy," he begged. "Don't say it. You'll break yourself up…"

"Because I'm crying?" she asked, defiantly. "Hal, discovering that he really is dead can't hurt me half as much as the torture of not knowing. And as long as this doubt gnaws at me, I'll be a river of pain dammed forever from the sea. The dam *will* break if I don't relieve the pressure."

"Then let *me* look!" he exclaimed. "There's no use in burning such a ghastly picture into your mind…"

"Don't be afraid of that," she said. "For eleven years I've burned a picture of him into my mind—ten years while I worshipped him from a distance, and one since I told him I loved him. No other picture can replace that one. I can take it, Hal, I'm no baby."

"You're crying like one," he said, and regretted the words instantly. "I'm sorry, Kathy. I didn't mean that. I'm a fool…" His voice broke and he stopped speaking.

She reached out and touched her cool fingers to his face. He stood still while they explored. He didn't flinch when she found the wetness.

"Hal," she said. "You're good. Too good to get into trouble because of me. Go now, Hal—I'll finish the job alone."

He hefted the crowbar in his left hand. "No," he said roughly. "I'm going to take this tomb apart, stone for stone, and if he's in there, I'm going to take the Capitol Building apart right afterward!" He strode on through the gloom of the marble monument to seek the hero whose real heroism had never even been told, whose life had been forfeited by the cowardice of a nation's government. Kathleen followed behind him, clutching his right hand with her left.

They reached the rail around the sunken marble mausoleum and Orson halted. "Over you go," he whispered. "I'll let you down and you can drop the last foot or so. It's only eight feet…" He put down the crowbar, and it clanged loudly against the floor.

Kathleen clambered over the rail. He grasped both her wrists and lowered her gently, leaning over as far as he could. Then, with a whispered warning, he released his grip. He heard her soft sandals slap against the floor, and knew that she hadn't lost her balance.

"Here I come," he said, picking up the crowbar.

In an instant he stood beside her in the gloom and fumbled in his pocket for the black-light spectacles necessary to give them vision. She put on a pair, and as he donned his, she snapped on the black-light flash. Without the glasses, nothing would have been visible at all in the impenetrable darkness. An eerie reddish-glow seemed to fill the chamber. He turned to look at her. She stood stiffly, staring at the huge marble coffin in the center of the circular floor. Even in the weird light he could see that her face was starkly white.

He clenched his fist so tightly that the nails bit into his palm, and turned almost savagely toward the coffin. She held the light while he placed the crowbar against the thin crack that marked the lid. The slab was tremendously heavy, but by fractional inches he forced the thin edge of the bar beneath it until enough of it was under the slab to give leverage. His first heave moved the slab not more than an inch. He tried it again, and once more he moved the slab a tiny bit.

"Can you do it?" Kathleen asked anxiously.

"It's a cinch you alone couldn't have," he grunted.

"I'd have smashed it," she said simply, "if it took me all night. I don't think anyone outside could hear what went on in here. It's almost soundproof."

"I hope so," he said, inching the bar under the slab once more. "It looks as though we'll be making plenty of noise before I get this off."

Ten sweating minutes later the slab had moved enough to show a thin black line of the interior of the outer coffin. Orson thrust the crowbar into it with a mighty heave. The muscles in his shoulders bunched as he strained against the bar. Then the lid slid aside as though it was greased and fell with a thunderous crash to the floor. The echoes were deafening in the vaulted chamber, then silence came once more.

They waited almost a full minute, listening for the sound of running footsteps, for an alarm; but no further sound came other than their hoarse breathing.

Kathleen thrust the light over the edge of the sarcophagus. "The coffin," she gasped. "It's there!"

"Of course," he said, almost savagely. "It would be. And it's going to be a devil of a job to open it. It's metal, and it'll be bolted shut. I only hope the wrenches I've brought will fit…"

He tried them one by one, then grunted as he found one that worked. He began loosening the first bolt…

An hour later he sank back, his hands bleeding. "There, that's the last one," he gasped, "but I'll have to rest a moment. I haven't got the strength left to lift that cover…"

Kathleen laid the flash on the floor and leaned over the coffin.

"Kathy!" said Orson sharply. "Don't…"

But with one superhuman heave, she lifted the metal cover. It crashed aside, pinging as though a thousand gongs had been clashed together. Orson clapped his hands over his ears, then took them off. He looked at Kathleen, who was peering into the coffin.

Suddenly she screamed. Again and again she screamed, ear piercing shrieks that penetrated his eardrums with more intensity than had the noise of the metal coffin lid.

He leaped forward, grasped her in his arms and pulled her away from the coffin.

"Kathy, come away. Don't look any more…"

Her screams stopped and she whirled on him, sobbing shrilly. "Hal, he's…*he's not there. The coffin's empty*…Don't you understand? He's not dead at all; *he's alive!*"

"Oh God," said Hal Orson, folding her trembling body in his arms. "Oh God!"

As he stood there, holding the sobbing girl tightly, his mind went back to that memorable day when the "luck of Suicide Martin Brand" had become almost a legend with the Interplanetary Patrol. They had heard it all over his transmitter, which, in the heat of battle, he had forgotten to turn off. They had heard him screaming his defiance at his enemies while he plunged in for his suicidal attack against impossible odds, accompanied by the roar of Wagner's immortal *Die Walküre* dinning at them out of their loudspeakers from the music tape he habitually carried into battle with him…

## CHAPTER TWO

"COME and get me, boys! If you can—!"

Martin Brand clenched one space-browned fist around the fighter's throttle and threw the ship into a screaming, roaring bank that ended in a terrific dive straight down, parallel with the breath-taking forty-thousand feet of cliff that was one side of the Liebnitz Mountains. With his other hand he pressed a switch on the control panel—a switch that had all the earmarks of having been crudely installed by one who was not a mechanic.

There was a faint hum, then from a speaker mounted over his head carne a burst of music.

Brand grinned as the strains of Wagner's inspired music dinned in his ears. He turned up the volume still further, until the roar of the music drowned out the drone of his rockets.

"Now come on, you lousy ambushers!" he roared.

Behind the ship against the rocky wall of the Liebnitz, a brilliant, soundless puff of light momentarily erased the inky moon-shadows at the mountain's foot.

"Missed!" exclaimed Brand triumphantly. "And you had me boxed!"

Suddenly, across his sights flashed a hurtling dot. Brand tripped his guns. Once again the bright light puffed, this time as one of Brand's shells exploded in the hull of the enemy ship.

"That's it!" screamed Brand. "The luck of 'Suicide' Martin Brand. Back on Earth I'm a legend, but right here, I'm a damn fool—a fool even the devil won't kill."

There was something bitter in Brand's tone as he shouted aloud over the crash of the magnificent Siegfried music, which was filling the control room of the tiny fighter rocket. There was bitter recklessness in the thrust of his hand as he bore the throttle over hard and sent the flier zooming up again in a heart-bursting maneuver.

The fire of the remaining three pirates—the thought of the word pirate brought an angry flash to Brand's eyes—converged on the Lunar floor over which he'd been, and then, suddenly, they were below him and in line with his sights as he looped over at the top of his upward rush.

Once again those brown fingers clenched, and this time a spray of shells vomited outward toward his enemies. Not just one lucky potshot, but a barrage with all six forward-guns.

Brilliance blinded him as thirty-six magnesium-atomics burst all around the diving ships trapped in his sights. When the light faded, he saw another ship dropping in a mass of fragments toward the desolate surface below. The other two were streaking desperately across the sea bottom, crater-hopping like mad, to put distance between them and the demon fighter who had so recklessly and amazingly escaped the perfect "box" ambush they had laid for him along the slopes of the Liebnitz.

Without pausing, Brand lanced his ship after them. Gray lava swept under the belly of his flier with a blur of motion. With a grim, set grin on his lips, he centered the crosshairs on the flames of the laggard's rockets. His fingers pressed delicately. Six shells "ringed" the ship, blasting it into fragments that showered down even as Brand's flier tore through the expanding gas of the explosion.

It was then that the surviving ship made its fatal mistake. At the range that now existed, the pirate might have escaped had its pilot continued in a straight line. Instead he shot his ship outward into space in an attempt to flee the satellite.

Brand's pursuing ship flared across the heavens. He instantly computed the angle of intersection, then waited, squinting his eyes. The pirate ship sped up into range of his guns...

Ten seconds later the fight was over. The wreck of the last pirate ship twisted madly as it hurtled down to a soundless crash on the airless sea-bottom.

Brand slacked speed, bore his ship around, and then brought it to a long, gliding landing near the wreckage.

And as he did so, a rocket flared beyond the wrecked ship. A tiny one-man escape rocket looped over a crater rim and streaked toward the horizon. Brand cursed.

"Damn! He got out before she crashed."

There was no chance of taking-off in time to catch the speedy little ship, so he switched on his communicator and roared into it.

"Run, you rat! And when you get home, tell your boss I'll get him sooner or later. The next time he tries to trap me, tell him to bring out his whole damn fleet!"

There was a faint hum in the receiver, and Brand snapped off his recorder, which was still blasting out the music of his favorite selection.

A voice came faintly from the speaker. Brand turned up the volume to its peak. With a crackling of static, but still quite clearly, the voice spoke.

"You never could hang on to anything, Martin Brand," came the voice, dripping with mockery. "Not even a girl. And the next time we meet, you won't be so lucky. I'll bring you in and you can give the boss your own messages."

There was a sudden snap and the hum faded from the speaker. The man in the escape rocket had cut off his radio.

But Martin Brand sat as though frozen, only the static of empty space breaking the silence inside his fighter. Only static; until his voice cracked out in a hoarse whisper that, had it become flesh and blood, would have been incarnate hate.

*"Jeffry Killian!"*

Again and again through Martin Brand's head echoed the words he had just heard. *You could never hang on to anything, Martin Brand. Not even a girl.* And as they repeated themselves over and over, another voice whispered in his mind...a voice as soft and musical as a summer breeze in a forest; cool, alluring, sweet. It whispered in his mind and carried him back over ten long years...

# CHAPTER THREE

"I love you, Martin. Oh so very much…"

Martin Brand crushed the slim girl's form to him as he kissed her yielding lips, passionately, tenderly, adoringly.

"We're going to be so happy, Estelle," he said. "Just wait till you see the home I've built for you. It's the coziest thing on three planets…"

"I can hardly wait," she said. "And I'll treasure everything in it. You've worked and fought so long and so hard to get it…"

"Just for you," he put in.

"Just for me?" she questioned coyly. "You've only known me five months. Couldn't it just as well have been any other girl?"

He clutched her to him.

"No, I've known you ever since I was old enough to know there could be anything like you on Earth. I've pictured you in my mind since almost the first time I rocketed a ship into space, a raw kid in the Interplanetary Patrol. I don't think there could have been a little home if you hadn't really existed."

"You dear," she said softly. "You idealistic darling."

He fished in his pocket, showed her the deed to their home to be, and for many moments they read it together.

"I've got to go now," he said then. "But I'll see you tomorrow morning at the spaceport. Then we'll walk up to Commander Wilson and get tied up in glorious style. Great old man, Commander Wilson. Not a man in the universe I'd rather rocket with. He gave me official orders to let him do the officiating."

"It'll be wonderful," she breathed.

Again he kissed her, and left.

"Commander wants to see you," said Brand's roommate when he reached his quarters. "Probably wants to make sure you've got the ring."

Brand grinned. He put his fingers into his watch pocket, removed a tiny box and flipped it at the rocketeer.

"From now on, Hal, it's your worry. You're best man, you know. And if I haven't a ring when Commander Wilson calls for it, there'll be one member of the Orson family who'll rocket no more."

"Take more than a Brand to stop an Orson," the rocketeer tossed at Brand's back, which was retreating through the doorway.

Brand knocked at Commander Wilson's door and waited. A gruff voice answered and he went in. He closed the door behind him, saluted sharply.

"Lieutenant Brand reporting as ordered, sir," he said.

Commander Wilson's space-tanned face appeared rather red in the glow of the desk light before him.

"Never mind the formality, son," he said. "Sit down. I've got some things to say to you."

He fussed around at some papers on his desk for a moment, while Brand seated himself and waited.

"Damned nuisance," fumed the commander. "Just when I wanted a vacation…"

Brand leaned forward, startled.

"We haven't been ordered out?" he questioned anxiously.

"Not immediately. But we leave in four days. You'll have a very short honeymoon, lad. Three days."

Brand looked disappointed, then he stiffened.

"We can arrange it, sir. If this thing's what I think it is, it's more important. We can continue the honeymoon later. After, all, we'll have a long time to be married."

Wilson chuckled.

"That's youth for you—think the honeymoon will never end. Well, I hope it doesn't, lad, because…" the commander sobered "…maybe the next ten years are going to be tough ones."

"The Martians?"

"Yes. The latest report comes from Luna. It seems a party of Martian scientists have obtained permission from the Lunarian government to conduct archeological explorations on the dark side. Archeology my foot. The dirty snakes are scouting the territory for military purposes."

"You mean you think Senator Beasley is right? That Mars intends to invade Earth?"

Commander Wilson grunted.

"I'm a soldier," he said. "I can see a million reasons why Mars should want to invade us, and *how* they could do it. Those damned pacifists keep prating about 41 million miles of space being a bulwark of natural defense. Bulwark, my hat! It's just a matter of coasting. What they really need is a base of operations near us…and that base is the moon."

"What are our orders?" asked Brand.

"Unofficial," said Wilson. "Senator Beasley and the President aren't asleep. We're to 'scout' beyond inter-planetary limits and keep our eyes open, but damn it, that isn't enough. Sooner or later we're going to have to institute a secret-service unit which will work entirely on its own risk—a body that can fight it out freelance and be prepared to take the rap if caught…"

"Count me in on that, Commander," said Brand swiftly. "I…"

"Not a chance." Wilson shook his head. "That'll be for single men only. It's too much of a suicide job. For instance, if the Lunarians nabbed one of these operatives, he'd probably be liable to life imprisonment, or even shot as a spy, and our government would have to deny him altogether. In fact, he'd forfeit his citizenship when he went into the service."

"You talk as though this service were already in existence."

"Not yet. But let's talk about that wedding tomorrow. Has she picked out a ring…?"

A confused babble of voices drifted across the take-off platform of the Space Patrol landing field. Brilliantly uniformed rocketeers stood chatting with lovely girls, and behind them loomed the tremendous mass of the blasting pit's metal—and—concrete walls. The morning sun was shining brightly, and beneath an arbor of flowers stood Commander Wilson, waiting. Before him stood a double line of officers of the Space Patrol, wearing their dress swords. At the far end of the line stood Martin Brand and Hal Orson.

Brand was fidgeting nervously, peering often toward the gates of the landing field, which yawned to the highway outside. It was here the limousine that would bring Estelle Carter and her bridesmaids was scheduled to appear.

"This thing's twisted," said Orson. "Isn't it supposed to be the groom who traditionally keeps the bride waiting?"

Brand grinned faintly.

"She's worth waiting for, Hal. But if she doesn't come soon, I'll need a fresh collar…"

Ten minutes passed, and Commander Wilson moved back into the shade of the arbor. Orson's face took on a sober look, and every few minutes he fumbled in his jacket pocket wherein reposed the ring for which he was responsible.

The purr of an atomic motor came from the road beyond the fence, and Brand stood erect. The line of officers snapped to attention; white gloves went to sword hilts in readiness.

A messenger's cycle swept in through the gate in a swirl of dust. Its rider dismounted, propped up his machine and strode forward.

"Lieutenant Martin Brand?" he asked.

Brand stepped forward.

"Here."

Brand took the message the boy handed him, while Orson tossed the lad a coin.

"Something wrong, Martin?" asked Orson while Brand scanned the message he had removed from the envelope.

Brand's face went white as the words bit into his brain…

*Congratulate us. Estelle and I will be married by the time you read this. No hard feelings. The best man won. Jeffry Killian.*

He didn't hear Orson's repeated question. He stood there, a blood-red haze before his eyes, a roar in his head. Slowly his fingers curled into a white-knuckled fist, crushing the paper into a ball. Then they relaxed and the paper fell to the ground. Unseeing, unhearing, oblivious of the tense silence that hung over the landing field, he strode through the gate toward his car.

He didn't hear the curse that Hal Orson let loose as he picked up and read the message. Hal Orson was too enraged to notice the pink cheeks, which he caused to appear on some of the girl attendants, and tensed jaws on the part of their escorts. The curse was echoed by Commander Wilson in modified form as he read the sheet from Orson's hand.

"The skunk! The no-good, rotten rat!"

As he strode through the gate, whispered words formed on Brand's lips.

*"She ditched me,"* he said. "Ditched me for a dare-devil space-racer. Eloped! And she only went out with him once…"

His hand whipped inside his jacket, tore out the deed to the little house. He ripped it into fragments and threw it to the winds. And then he laughed, harshly and loudly.

There was a heavy silence in the room. Hal Orson fumbled aimlessly with the television set, as a variety of scenes faded in and out on the screen.

"We take-off at noon tomorrow," he said abstractly. "Be good to get into space again. I've got a bellyful of this inaction…"

Brand sat on the bed, looking dazed. He remained silent. Orson looked at him, shook his head, frowned, then returned his attention to the televisor. More scenes flashed on. A newscaster's face appeared. His voice droned…

*Martian war spread to another front on the red world today, when the Syrtis armies attacked tiny Malvia without warning. Tank columns followed initial attack by rocket-bombers and smashed through Malvian defenses at three vital points…*

The announcer's voice went on and his features were replaced at times by maps illustrating the areas under discussion. Then he launched into an account of local news.

*Early this morning the wrecked racing-rocket of the famed inter-planetary-racer, Jeffry Killian, was found on the Maine coast, half sub-merged. A young woman, tentatively identified as Miss Estelle Carter of New York, was taken from the crackup in serious condition…*

Orson turned slowly to face Martin Brand, who was rising to his feet, a stricken expression on his face as he faced the televisor screen. On the screen now was a view of the wreck, a grimly shattered object washed by foamy seas as the wind roared in a gale from the Atlantic. The announcer's voice continued:

*…and has been removed to the Community Hospital at Boston. The body of Jeffry Killian has not been located as yet, and it is believed that it may be lost in the sea, thrown clear of the wreckage.*

Hal Orson snapped off the television and tossed Brand his coat.

"Come on Martin, we'd better get started. I'll rocket you up there in my speedster."

Brand's face was pale, and…his browned hand was trembling as he caught the coat.

"Thanks, Hal," he said. "But don't spare the fireworks. I've got to get to her before…before…"

"We will," promised Orson. "We'll be there in a half-hour."


"She isn't badly injured physically," said the doctor, "bruises and contusions, a broken arm, and head injuries. We had to operate on her head as soon as we got her here—pressure on the brain. Would have killed her in another two hours. Unfortunately, a bone chip on the inside of the skull had penetrated a portion of the brain, causing damage to an extent, which we can't predict at the moment. It may be…"

"How's she now?" asked Brand tensely. "Can I see her?"

The doctor shrugged.

"Yes, you can see her, but it isn't exactly—well, pretty. You see, she's violently insane."

Brand went white.

"You mean…?"

"Perhaps. There's not much hope that she'll regain her sanity. There's been some sort of mental shock also. Perhaps the sight of her…companion drowning while she was powerless to help him."

"I want to see her," said Brand, tight-lipped.

The doctor led the way down the corridor to a small room. Brand entered first. He halted as he saw the figure on the bed.

"She's strapped down!" he exclaimed.

On the bed lay Estelle Carter, her legs and arms strapped to the bed, a leather strap across her breast. Her head was heavily bandaged and one arm was in a cast. Her eyes were open, and they stared directly into Brand's with an intense glare that stopped his lips with shock.

"Look at the tin soldier boy," she jeered. "I hate you, I hate you, I hate everybody! You've got stars in your eyes…"

In startling change she recoiled, fearful, eyes dilated.

"Stars!" she shrieked. "They're in your eyes, and they're getting bigger. The whole sky is full of them. Running races, that's what they are. Racers. And cowards too. They aren't really racing—they're running away…ooohhhh-hh!"

Her voice ended in a high-treble scream, filled with utter terror combined with horrible hate. She tossed convulsively on the bed.

"The fool, he thought I loved him. He got a deed to a nasty little shack… Get away from me. You've got racers in your eyes."

Martin Brand recoiled. Then he moaned and a shudder shook his big shoulders. Abruptly he wheeled, ran from the room, colliding with Hal Orson whose face was white and tense.

Outside, sobs tore from Brand's throat, while Orson gripped his arm tightly and held it.

Commander Wilson extended his hand and shook that of Martin Brand, soberly but with feeling.

"Welcome to the Special Service," he said. "From now on you are a free agent. You will receive your instructions from me only. And your area will be 24B-Luna. Your identity has been established as Robert Wales, political criminal. No one connects Robert Wales with Martin Brand, the ace of the Interplanetary Patrol. As Robert Wales you have no rights as a citizen, although none can deny that you are still an

Earthman. All of your actions will be those of a renegade. But your job is to smash the plot that is brewing on Luna. Mars must not be allowed to establish a fifth column there, nor to invade. Until the 'powers that be' realize our danger, we must work in the dark. If you get into trouble, your government will deny you."

Brand nodded.

"I know. It's all right. I have nothing to lose." His voice was dull.

Commander Wilson poured a brandy from his private stock.

"Drink this," he said. "And snap out of it. You've got a job to do. And you've done a noble thing by setting aside all of your savings as a fund for Estelle. She'll be taken care of. But don't let it make you bitter. There are other women…"

"Not in this service," snapped Brand. "Remember what you told me once before?"

"Sure, but…"

"That's the way it suits me," said Brand. "And as far as my job is concerned, the Martians will wish I'd never been born."

"I'm sure they will," said Wilson, a troubled look in his eyes, "but don't be reckless. A dead agent is of no use to us, you know."

A flinty grin crossed Brand's face.

"I don't die easily, Commander," he said. "But neither will I live long enough to be a sucker again."

## CHAPTER FOUR

Martin Brand stared unseeingly across the wastes of the lunar plain, which stretched back toward the towering heights of the Liebnitz from which he had just come. Still ringing through his brain were those words he had spoken ten long years before. They had been the basis for the Martin Brand the solar system now knew as "Suicide" Martin Brand, the luckiest man alive—and the most daring.

Ten years ago, his life had been blasted into a terrible bitterness. Now, when he thought the wound healed by time, a voice had come out of the ether from a crater-hopping little escape ship, tearing it wide open once more. A voice that he hated, a voice he had thought he'd never hear again.

"He isn't dead." Brand's voice rang with hate and shock in the tiny confines of his little pursuit ship. *"Jeffry Killian is still alive!* He didn't drown when his ship cracked up…"

The full significance of it jolted home in his mind.

"The rat cracked her up, thought she was dead, and ran out on her like a coward. And she *knew.* She was insane, but she still remembered he'd run out on her. And later—he must have known it—hearing that she was insane, he never came back. Let her shift for herself…" Martin Brand's face writhed in an old hate, now reborn to full growth in a terrible manner.

"I'll get you, Killian," he swore. *"I'll get you, if I have to tear the whole Moon apart!"*

Beneath the savage pressure of his fingers, the pursuit rocket roared up from the age-old dust of the lunar plain, shot over the wrecks of the ships he had shot down, and out into space toward Earth.

Three days later, Martin Brand, dressed in the rough garb of a prospector, peered from the porthole of the limping freighter which was settling down past the high rim of the crater that exactly centered the side of the Moon eternally hidden from Earth. He watched with interest as darkness settled around the ship. The gloom became deeper as the ship sank into the bowels of this pockmarked world.

As he watched, the admonishing words of Commander Wilson rang in his memory. *It's a tough hunch you're playing, my boy. If it really was Jeffry Killian you saw, then something is going on inside Luna that's no good at all. Whatever you encounter will be strictly your own funeral if it blows up in your face. Good luck, son. Somehow, soon, we've got to smash that Martian infiltration, or it's curtains for Earth.*

Yes, it would be strictly his funeral—because now he wasn't Martin Brand. He was Robert Wales, and Robert Wales was an outlaw on Earth. He'd lost his citizenship because of seditious acts. Oh, yes, the rest of the solar system would accept him without much question. His wasn't a universal criminal act. In fact, much of the solar system would secretly approve of an Earthman who was a seditionist…Mars especially, and perhaps Venus. On Luna he would use still another name (he'd selected Edgar Barnes) because Luna was anxious about Mars; and curried favor from Earth. And too, she was a bit irritated because Earth politicians stuck bull-headedly to their isolationist policy. Luna also resented being a "buffer" between Earth and Mars without getting credit for it

If Luna discovered that Edgar Barnes was Robert Wales she might deport him, certainly not to Earth, but very likely to Venus. So Martin Brand intended to play his dual role with all the cunning—and uncanny luck—that was his.

The freighter was dropping now into an illuminated area. Light came from below, and suddenly with the shock that it always brings to persons making a first descent into the hollow world, the breath-taking spectacle of the cavern's immensity opened out beneath him. There was a city there. A modern Lunar city, built, precariously it seemed, on a terrific slope. How it could have remained there was an incredible mystery.

Brand shifted his body, and the mystery was a mystery no longer; for he almost fell, with a new shift of balance from a new center of gravity. The precipitous slope on which the city stood became a flat plain, and the black hole of the crater through which the ship, now emerged shifted from its former vertical appearance to a low-slanting shaft that bore off at an angle.

A moment later he adjusted himself to the sudden change in direction, found the new "down" and regained his equilibrium. And when he had accomplished it, the ship shuddered with the contact of its faulty landing in the rocket cradles at the city spaceport.

As he walked down the gangplank, reeling slightly with the unaccustomed light gravity in spite of his leaded shoes, Brand wanted to laugh aloud. He stopped himself as he heard several others laughing boisterously, then he saw them peering around with a foolish look on their faces. There had been nothing to laugh at. Brand grinned faintly at their discomfiture, realizing the cause of the unseemly mirth...oxygen. The atmosphere of this inner-lunar world was artificial and richer in pure oxygen than that of Earth. Its too-swift stimulation often caused this reaction when first breathed into lungs unaccustomed to it.

Brand stopped grinning as he saw a girl standing just outside the gate of the spaceport looking at him with what he was certain was startled recognition. But she was a perfect stranger to him, and he frowned. Her face now, as she saw him looking at her, went cold and emotionless and casual.

Brand walked over toward her, seemed about to pass without further notice, then whirled upon her.

"Do I know you?" he asked abruptly...

It seemed to him that she drew in her breath just a bit too sharply. "No," she said in a low voice, staring straight at him. "You don't."

"Wrong reaction," he said flatly. "You're supposed to say: 'Can't you think up a more original approach than that—go fry your hide.' I know I don't know you. But I'd swear you know me."

She continued to look at him levelly.

"What is your name?" she asked. "If you're well-known enough, I might have heard of you."

"Edgar Barnes," he answered. "Prospector."

"No," she said. "I don't know you."

She turned and walked away. Brand watched her retreating back a moment, noting the lilting sway of her body, the grace of each step, the proud carriage of her head. He saw too the rich red-gold of her hair, and remembered that her eyes had been a startling deep blue. He had noticed also that her lips had been anything but forbidding, even tightly drawn as they had been in what he could not certainly identify as deception.

*Had* she recognized him, or hadn't she? *Was* she concealing an initial betrayal of such recognition, or had she, like himself, been surprised at the laughter caused by the oxygen in the air? But *he* hadn't laughed; why look at him?

He shrugged, turned and strode through the city streets.

Ahead of him he saw a brilliantly lighted cafe. Its neon lights proclaimed it as the "Star Club." Parked in front of it were sleek aero-cabs and several fast, low-slung compression flyers.

Brand nodded to himself.

"There's where I'll find some of the big boys. Perfect front for intrigue."

He turned in at the entrance and was halted by a doorman.

"You can't go in dressed like that."

Brand grinned.

"Call the manager," he said, "unless you'd rather take this ten-spot yourself. I've got a little to unload…"

The doorman snatched the bill Brand handed him, grinned back, and said, "Sure. The boss'll understand when I give him the sign. And thanks…"

Brand followed a waiter to a small table to one side, seated himself and ordered a drink. Then he sat quietly, listening to the haunting strains of the Lunarian stringed orchestra which was wailing its odd cadences for the dancing of the couples swaying voluptuously on the dance floor.

Lunarian dances were the ultimate in sensuous expression. Brand snorted, and downed his drink in a gulp when it came. The waiter lifted his eyebrows, and Brand ordered another, loudly.

Several men nearby looked at him, studied him a moment.

One of them got up and sauntered over. He was dressed in evening attire, and immaculately groomed, but there was a queer tightness of his suit around the chest, and Brand's eyes narrowed slightly as the fellow sat down opposite him. There was a shoulder holster under his arm, and a steam gun in it. There was no mistaking that telltale tightness, for Brand.

"Prospector?" queried his guest.

"Of sorts." Brand shrugged. "Just landed. Thought I'd try my hand at the caves."

"Bad business, those caves," said the stranger affably. "Takes a good man to browse around in 'em. Never prospected myself, but I've hunted lu-bats in those caves. Incidentally, my name's Ormandy. Saw you down that drink, which is exactly how I feel at the moment. Mind if I join you in the next?"

"Why should I? Maybe you can give me some dope on the caves—that's worth sharing a drink."

The waiter arrived, and strangely enough he had the other man's drink on his tray.

"They know me here," explained Ormandy. "When I sit down at a table, any table, they stick my drink in front of me."

"Not a bad thing," grinned Brand, "saves time."

He lifted his glass, then held it rigidly in his fingers for a moment. There, behind Ormandy, across the room, was the girl Brand had accosted at the spaceport. There was no mistaking the red sheen of that lovely hair. And once more she was staring at him. This time there was no recognition, just a studied attention that held him motionless with surprise for an instant.

"What's up?" queried Ormandy, "See a lu-bat?"

He turned to stare in the direction Brand was looking, and raised his eyebrows.

"Say," he said in approval. "Don't blame you for looking. She's strictly inner-world!"

Brand recovered himself hastily.

"Yeah," he agreed, tossing his drink over his shoulder into a potted palm as the girl looked away. Ormandy's head was still turned. Brand smacked his lips and put his glass down.

Ormandy drank his, then leaned on the table.

"You haven't introduced yourself," he said. "Not curious, but I ought to have a handle to hang on you. Any one'll do."

Brand grinned.

"Ed Barnes," he said. "Just an ordinary name, but it's done me this long, I guess you can use it too."

"Y'know," said Ormandy. "For a minute I thought you were somebody else, but I guess it's that deep coat of space-tan you've got. Either you've been prospecting the airless asteroids, or been rocketing around space for a spell."

"Both," said Brand. "In fact, this is the first air outside of a tank I've breathed in a long time, except on the freighter that brought me here, I shipped on from a space station out of New York, intended to go to Earth, but decided against it. I've always wanted to try the Luna caves."

Ormandy reached carelessly into his vest. When his hand came out, he palmed a small steam pistol. The tiny opening in the barrel was all that was visible to Brand as he stared at the hand. He didn't move a muscle.

Across the room a nattily dressed American space-lieutenant lifted his voice in a popular space song which the orchestra was playing at the moment. His voice rang out clearly, but slightly tipsily in the quiet that seemed to have fallen over the room.

*"Let me tell you of a girl*
*I met among the stars.*
*Her eyes are blue as Rigel;*
*Her lips as red as Mars."*

"Ten years ago," said Ormandy softly, I stood in line at a wedding ceremony, my sword at the ready. I was prepared to add my weapon to the arch through which a young couple was to walk in a few moments. But the wedding never came off. It seems that the man who was to form half of that team was being jilted…"

Brand's face tightened just a trifle and he looked hard at the man across the table from him, but said nothing. Instead, queerly, the song's second verse registered in his ears, and he listened to it as he studied Ormandy's eyes.

*"Nowhere in all the system*
*You'll find a girl like she;*
*And you can bet your ray gun*
*That she's the one for me!"*

Ormandy's voice went on:

"That man was just a lieutenant in the space-patrol then. I was also one, but I had other interests. They had something to do with a situation that was only beginning then. I didn't know at the time that the man who was being jilted would be so bitter about it that he'd become a thorn in my side later on. Of course the interests which I planned were then in their infancy. Today they are quite well advanced…"

*"Her hair is like the ghostweed*
*That drifts on Venus' sea.*
*From top to toe a' figure*
*As perfect as can be."*

"It would be a shame to let any possible harm come to them now. So that is why you are looking into the muzzle of a very efficient little steam gun right now, Mr. Martin Brand. 'Suicide' Martin Brand, I believe is the popular designation, which, at the moment, is quite appropriate indeed."

"Perhaps," agreed Brand. "I've gotten to depend on my luck so much that I often stick my head into the lion's mouth like this. Someday it's going to make me careless."

"Like now?" questioned Ormandy softly.

"Maybe. But how'd you spot me?"

Ormandy frowned.

"Recognized you, of course," he snapped.

"That's a lie," said Brand. "In the first place you've never seen me before, and in the second place you never were at any wedding. Every one of the boys in that line, with or without swords were my friends. All except the one who ran off with my girl, cracked up with her, and ran off like a rat, leaving her to a life of insanity. And thirdly, I don't look like Martin Brand at all. I'm a mess of plastic."

Ormandy looked at him a moment, then he laughed contemptuously.

"You're smart, Brand and a liar. But so what? Right now you're going to walk out of here with me, climb into the black aero-cab directly in front, and sit tight. The driver knows me quite well. In fact, you might say he's a friend. He'll never remember having taken a fare anywhere tonight, especially a prospector named Ed Barnes, whom nobody'll ever see again. Not when his body drops into Black Hole."

"Black Hole?"

"That's the crater that goes nowhere that anybody's ever been able to discover—and came back alive."

"Oh, I see."

Brand's eyes strayed a split second over Ormandy's shoulder, and saw with surprise that the girl was gone. Her drink stood on the table at which she'd been seated. It was untouched.

"Get up," ordered Ormandy. "The drinks are on me. Just walk out."

Brand got up. He nodded casually to the doorman as he walked past. Ormandy was a few paces behind. Outside, Brand waited.

"That cab," indicated Ormandy.

Brand glanced around carefully. In a doorway to one side of the brilliantly lit marquee of the Star Club he saw a glint of red. There was a slight hiss, a tiny white lance of light came from the doorway, and ended in the temple of his captor. Ormandy sighed, slid gently to the walk, and dropped the steam gun from his nerveless palm.

Brand stooped, scooped it up, whipped open the door of the aero-cab, and trained the weapon on the startled driver.

"Start going places," he snapped. "Fast!"

He leaped in, turned to see the figure of the mysterious girl in the doorway. He saw her return a steam gun to her bodice, then disappear into the Star Club's side door once more. On the walk before the cafe the body of Ormandy lay like an inkblot. For the instant no one was in sight, then the doorman came running out, and several pedestrians began to converge on the corpse. Then the scene vanished from view as the aero-cab lifted, shot into the darkness over the city.

## CHAPTER FIVE

The girl sitting in the easy chair in the solarium was staring blankly at the landscape that spread out before her beyond the wide-flung windows admitting the morning sun and air.

Behind her an ornate radio played softly, rendering the symphonic tone poem, *Rakastava,* of Sibelius. Its notes were muted, low, distant. They were soothing, restful. And the girl who sat so still seemed lost in them. Her eyes were fixed on nothing, her body relaxed. Yet, beneath the calm exterior there was a strange tension that betrayed itself in tiny, tense wrinkles around her eyes, on the bridge of her nose, and especially in the nervous twitching of the fingers of one hand.

Moving softly, furtively around the room, an aproned girl dusted furniture with almost fearful industriousness. Often she glanced quickly at the quiet figure in the easy chair, then snatched her attention away again to return to her work.

Someone appeared in the doorway. The maid glanced up.

"Good morning," said the newcomer, drawing a brilliant robe around her figure, waiting expectantly for an answer. None came from the girl in the chair, but the maid rushed forward on tiptoe, one startled finger to her lips in an unmistakable gesture.

*"Quiet!"* she hissed. "Do you want to make her violent again?"

"Oh, shush, Olga," said the visitor, pushing back a lock of graying hair from her more than middle-aged face. "She isn't going to be violent. She's no more crazy than I am—or..." she fixed a stern glance on Olga's fear-ridden face, "...or you." Olga reddened, and returned flustered to her silent pursuit of dust that didn't exist. Under her breath she mumbled.

"Crazy? Miss Pennyfeather, you're *insane!*"

If Miss Pennyfeather heard, she gave no indication. Instead she walked over to the girl in the easy chair and sat down on the window ledge directly before her, craning her neck to bring her gaze directly into line with the girl's blank stare. For a long moment she peered.

"Good morning, Estelle," she said.

There was no answer. Miss Pennyfeather looked irritated. She inched herself more directly in line with Estelle Carter's gaze, rising to a half-sitting position that gave her the appearance of a poised scarecrow.

There was no evidence that Estelle saw her visitor. Miss Pennyfeather became more irritated. She reached out a hand to still the fingers of the girl's hand, then sat back again, and a judicious look crossed her face.

"It's that music," she decided. "It's too spiritless. We must have something with fire, something to wake us." She got up, walked over to the radio and snapped a switch.

"This is better. *The Ride of the Valkyries,* from *Die Walküre,* by Richard Wagner." She read the title with gusto. "This will brighten us up."

She inserted the record, snapped a new switch. Then she turned up the volume slightly and returned to her seat on the window ledge. She tossed a defiant stare at Olga, who had been standing disapprovingly in one position while Miss Pennyfeather launched her campaign for "brightening things up."

"Go about your work, Olga," she said sharply. "That radio is simply filthy with dust." She rubbed her fingers on her skirt with distaste.

Olga frowned and returned to the chair on which she had been working, but she cast an exploratory glance at the radio and squinted.

The strains of the Wagnerian music began swelling through the room, building up to crashing chords. Miss Pennyfeather sat patiently waiting for her "brightening up" efforts to take effect on her victim.


"Those stars keep racing around," said Estelle abstractedly. "And I hate racers."

Miss Pennyfeather lifted her eyebrows.

"Stars?" she asked. "Where do you see stars racing?"

Estelle's eyes focused on her visitor's face, as if she were seeing her for the first time.

"I *don't* see them," she said. *"He's* a star. A star racer. He's won so many medals. But he always runs away. He's a coward, and I hate him."

"Don't you love anybody?" asked Miss Pennyfeather.

"No. Men are such fools."

"Hasn't anybody ever loved you?"

Estelle laughed.

"Certainly…but I didn't love him. He wanted to buy a little house and tie me down in it. He was so old-fashioned. He knew how to kiss, and that's all I wanted…"

The girl's gaiety vanished suddenly, and she leaned forward in her chair. An anxious look came over her features.

"I hear his voice," she exclaimed.

Miss Pennyfeather frowned.

"The only men here are Doctor Allen and Doctor Deakin," she said, "and you couldn't hear any voices outside anyway. The music is getting too loud."

Estelle relaxed again, and her fingers resumed the twitching motion.

Behind them Olga neared the radio. She peered at it closely.

"Filthy with dust," she whispered. She began polishing it with her cloth, an ecstatic look in her eyes. Her fingers accidentally touched the volume control, turning it over to full strength...

With startling suddenness the music roared out deafeningly. The climactic chords of the tremendous selection shook the walls.

Estelle Carter leaped from her chair. Her shrill scream rocketed through the air, even above the blasting radio. Her face was a mask of shock and surprise and terror. She ran back and forth, as though seeking an escape, her hands clasped over her ears, and she screamed again and again.

"Martin! *Martin!*"

Miss Pennyfeather looked as though she'd been struck by lightning, Olga crumpled to the floor next to the radio, crying in hysteria.

Estelle shrieked once more, then fell to the floor in a faint.

Miss Pennyfeather leaped into action. With terror in her face, she rushed through the doorway, colliding with the form of Doctor Deakin. She recovered, and rushed on down the hall, passed Doctor Allen with averted eyes, and turned into her room.

"Turn off that radio!" shouted Doctor Allen, reaching the solarium. "Good God, there's no telling what this shock will do to Miss Carter."

The blasting thunder of the music was cut off abruptly, and only the sobs of the maid filled the room.

"Get Olga out of here, Deakin," directed Doctor Allen. "I'll take care of Miss Carter. I'm afraid this might be serious. It's enough to kill her, or cure her…"

Several days later the two men faced each other in their office.

"What's the verdict, Allen?"

Doctor Allen leaned back in his chair.

"Cured. Completely cured! That shock absolutely counteracted the one which deranged her mind in the accident. She's as sane as you or I, and she knows it. She has a fine mind, or she couldn't have taken the revelations of the past few days without suffering a breakdown. It's quite a shock to realize that you've been insane for ten years."

"You're going to release her?"

"Certainly. Fortunately she has quite a sum still in her fund, that is being turned over to her. I have no doubt but that she'll find a place for herself without difficulty. She's a clever girl—even brilliant. I've been amazed at the extent of her knowledge and her intelligence rating."

"You don't fear a relapse?" Allen shook his head.

"No," he said slowly, "I don't. There's something pretty solid in her mind. Perhaps the combination of those two shocks has accomplished something that might not otherwise have been possible. She's as cold and analytical as a mathematics machine. If anything, she's too sane. Her emotions are under a powerful mental control. What she really needs is the outside world. I might even hope that she'd fall in love, although the way she's constituted now, I'd hardly think that was possible. Anyway, she's leaving us today."

"Where's she going?"

"Says she has hopes of a business contact with a fellow named Jeffry Killian."

"Jeffry Killian! Why that's the man she cracked up with. He's dead—drowned in the wreck."

"Oh!" exclaimed Doctor Allen, startled. He settled back in his chair, a puzzled look on his face, then, after a moment, it cleared.

"That's too bad," he said, "but maybe it has its compensations. After all, sorrow is akin to love—it's an emotion. And that's what she needs. Once emotion returns to her she'll be a pretty fine woman. I think I'll just let her go, and find out about Killian for herself. She can certainly take the shock, and it might soften her nervous system up a bit."

"It might..." said his companion dubiously. "Perhaps it might..."

## CHAPTER SIX

Martin Brand poked the steam gun into the aero-car driver's back with a vicious jab.

"Was the guy back there your boss?"

"No. I'm just a taxi driver."

"You lie. I know all about this set-up, and I'm here to break it. I intend to break it!"

The driver turned half around.

"What set-up?" he asked. "I ain't in no set-up..."

"Keep on driving, and face front," ordered Brand grimly, "and make for the Black Hole. We've got a little date there."

He saw the red neck of the driver go pale.

"What you going to do?" he quavered.

"Kill you," said Brand laconically.

He saw the driver's knuckles go white on the steering wheel, but the face remained rigidly toward the front. The aero-cab drove on through the darkness beyond the city, through the artificial atmosphere of the great cavern.

Pockmarked everywhere were great black areas that betokened uninhabited areas, and bright spots that indicated cities. To one side, the side facing the sun, several bright spots indicated craters that extended straight through the crust, similar to the giant one, which provided the main access to the moon's interior down which Brand had come in the freighter.

Dimly, across the black void above them, paths of light indicated the sun's beams. In the windless interior, no dust floated, and dust motes did not break up the beams and make them the brilliant shafts they are in Earth caves.

Only opposite the crater through which the beams entered did the sun's rays add any appreciable light to this stygian inner-world. There, brilliant white spots outglowed the artificial light of cities, but were easily confused with the cities.

Brand knew had they been further out from the surface he could have seen the huge Black Hole that was their destination. It might be on the near up-curving horizon in almost any direction, and Brand felt with certainty that the driver of the aero-cab was *not* going toward it. He'd seen him cautiously, with extreme slowness, so as not to make it noticeable, change his course several times. And Brand knew this was just a means of determining if he, Brand, knew where the Black Hole was.

With an inner smile playing about his lips Brand waited, eyes and ears open, on the alert.

The driver indicated a black area just ahead.

"There is the beginning of the Black Hole crater," he said. "What do you intend to do with me now?"

"Go directly over it," Brand said, "and then drop down into it slowly."

The man complied, and the little vessel dropped slowly down in a direct vertical.

Brand seemed to be intently watching the crater walls, shrouded in blackness, but in reality, his attention was fixed on the driver. He saw the slow tensing of the tiny muscles in the fingers of his right hand as they drew near to a certain outcropping of rock that formed a rather wide ledge. Here was a dim glow, and Brand saw that even a space ship could land on the ledge with room to spare. But their aero-car was several hundred yards out from it, and descending very slowly.

Suddenly, Brand acted. He leaped forward, raised the steam gun, brought it down on the driver's head just as the man's right hand shot out toward a button on the dash. The driver uttered a little moan, slumped over the wheel. The aero-car began a whistling dive down into the crater darkness.

Brand wrestled the inert body away from the control seat and took over. In a moment he had halted the downward dive, bore the ship off in a slanting zoom away from the danger of crashing the walls, then hung for a moment, getting his bearings.

Above him was the landing ledge he had seen before. Certain that he hadn't lost the clue it had given him, Brand began to drop the ship slowly again. Into pitch darkness they went. Brand kept one ear cocked to the stertorous breathing of the driver, who was still unconscious. Any change in it would indicate returning consciousness.

Abruptly the aero-car bumped solid rock. Brand turned off the motors. A quick flash of the lights, on dim, showed that he had reached the floor of this particular pit. It was certainly not the Black Hole. In all, it was perhaps three miles deep, and small in diameter at the base. He placed a small package in the man's pocket, searched him for weapons, found none, and after a moment of thought left a small flashlight. It was a weak, two-celled affair, and its beam would penetrate the gloom only a few feet. He dragged the unconscious man from the cab.

Then Brand stepped back into the aero-cab and started up the shaft of the crater toward the ledge above.

He drove the ship silently down toward the far end of the great ledge landed in pitch darkness close to the crater wall, under a slight overhang of rock. There he turned off the motors and left the ship.

Slowly, he made his way through the inky blackness on foot, carefully feeling his way along the rocky wall, extending an exploratory foot forward before taking each step. He proceeded in this manner for nearly an hour.

The dim light on the ledge grew stronger, and suddenly Brand discovered the reason for it. Here and there, in patches on the rock wall, a dully-luminous paint had been splashed. His hunch had been right. The driver of the aero-cab had been intent on flashing on all the lights of his cab thereby attracting attention, and being rescued from his plight. He had firmly believed that Brand intended to kill him, and had tried to save his life—and in so doing had betrayed the hiding place of the men Brand was seeking.

Here in this pit, somewhere along this ledge, there must be an opening big enough to admit space ships. An opening big enough to be used as a base, for the fifth-column activities Brand sought to uncover and destroy.

Perhaps now, at last, he would come to grips with the master criminal, the Martian genius who was building up the secret springboard for an all-out offensive against Earth. The offensive that Earth authorities and Earth people alike scoffed at, because they denied the possibility of an invasion across 41,000,000 to 134,000,000 miles of space.

He went on, now able to see dimly in the phosphorescent glow of the luminous-paint splotches. He no longer had to feel his way, held his steam gun in readiness prepared for any surprise.

Here, he felt sure, judging from the covert actions of the aero-cab driver, he could expect to find sentries. At least he knew he'd find someone to whom a bright light would have meant apprehensive action.

Alert, he went on, his soles grinding softly in the sandy pumice of the ledge-floor. Before him he saw a black area in the cliff wall. It was a cavern opening and on both sides of it were groups of heavy boulders. Behind them several men could have hidden very easily.

Brand dropped down and crawled along on his belly, taking advantage of every possible concealment. There was no noise, but to Brand the scuff of his own body in the sand sounded almost thunderous.

It was with surprise that he stopped his progress and became rigidly immobile at the sight of a dark figure seated with his back against a rock. The man was smoking a cigarette, and the tip of it glowed red as he dragged on it. His face was illuminated, and Brand's pulse leaped.

A Martian!

He'd found the opening. There was no doubt that this was the hiding place of a part of the fifth-column Mars was establishing on Luna. This man was a guard. Across his knees was a long atom-rifle, one that could easily shoot down an aero-car at a distance of several miles. Brand knew the weapon, a deadly invention of Earth, which I had been stolen by spies and duplicated in Martian factories. It had been used to potent advantage in the Martian invasion of Callisto. It had telescopic sights that were so perfect, and had so great a range that even the astronomers marveled at them.

The Martian seemed certain that his duty was an unnecessary one. That an intruder would find this ledge or attempt to land on it was preposterous to him. Brand glanced out into the void of the interior of Luna, and saw that any ship without lights would be perfectly invisible against the black curtain. That is, unless it chanced to cross a spot of light that betokened a city on the other side, or blundered into one of the shafts of sunlight that lanced almost invisibly across the cavern. It was obvious that the guard had not seen the aero-cab descend. Nor could he see a light from the crater bottom, because it would be necessary for him to go directly to the ledge termination and peer over.

Slowly Brand crept forward, his gun in hand. The guard smoked his cigarette down, flicked it away into the darkness, then he climbed slowly to his feet. His seven feet of height towered over Brand, who froze motionless again. The guard relaxed the hold on his rifle, stretched his great shoulders and yawned.

Brand rose slowly to his feet and advanced. A pebble crunched beneath his feet.

The guard whirled, his gun came up with amazing swiftness, the muzzle pointing directly at Brand's body. Startled by the dexterity of the fellow's movements, Brand had time to do no more than press the trigger of his steam gun. A white lance leaped out, striking the Martian in the abdomen. The Martian doubled over in agony, but retained his footing, bringing his gun once more into line.

Brand shot again, swiftly, surely, and the steam lance ended its trail of death directly between the guard's eyes. Like an empty sack of brittle burlap, which refused to flatten out, the Martian's fragile body collapsed. He lay motionless on the pumice, dark blood oozing from the wound in his head.

"He wasn't so off-guard at that," muttered Brand. "And it wasn't so good for him. It cost him his life. If I could have sneaked by…"

But then he laughed.

"What am I feeling sorry for? These fellows intend to murder millions on Earth, if we give them the chance."

He stepped over to the body, searched it. He found nothing but a pack of cigarettes, which he pocketed, some matches, a second steam gun in a holster, and a belt of ammunition. He picked up the atom-gun, hefted its long length, then retraced his steps toward his ship some hundred yards, and cached his loot along the base of the cliff-wall.

He returned and lifting the Martian's body, he carried it to the edge of the ledge and hurled it over.

Then, all traces of his activities having been removed, he made his way into the black opening of the cave. As he rounded a bend, a source of illumination became visible, and he saw that ahead there was a broadening of the tunnel, plus several branching tunnels that led off at angles. Obviously, this was a complex system of caves and tunnels—an ideal hiding place for Martian agents and Lunarian fifth-columnists.

Brand crept forward, following the illumination, his nerves tense with caution. He progressed several hundred yards before the illumination became bright enough for him to follow without feeling for his footing. He could now see the rock underfoot, and he realized that this was no artificial illumination, but a natural glow that emanated from the rock itself.

So far he had seen no signs of the human occupancy that he sought, and his brows furrowed in puzzlement. Why bury themselves so deeply? Obviously, farther ahead, there was a huge cave, lighted with phosphorescence, but peering at the tunnel floor, Brand could see no traces of any passage through the sand and scattered pumice. In fact, his own footprints showed clearly and distinctly.

Brand halted. Something was wrong about this. If the enemy used this tunnel as a hideout, they either carefully obliterated their trail, or entered by another route. Perhaps the right way through was one of those diverging tunnels behind him? …But they had not been illuminated. The light had drawn him here.

Brand went ahead more slowly, came into the main cavern, a large place, perhaps several miles in diameter. One glance was enough to tell him it was entirely empty. There was no possible place in this huge lava bubble where anything as large as a rat could have hidden.

"Wrong trail!" exclaimed Brand in annoyance. His voice echoed and re-echoed from the walls of the cave with startling repetition. Brand clenched his lips shut in tight alarm, as those sounds might echo for miles through these tunnels.

When silence descended again, Brand took a last look. He saw a tiny black opening in the wall several hundred feet away, and walked toward it cautiously. It led into pitch darkness.

Was this the way? Was he on the right trail at that?

He stepped inside, walked on into gloom that grew blacker, until with a turning of the passage it became complete. Once more he was forced to feel his way along. After a time, the sound of his footsteps ceased abruptly to echo back to him, and became almost soundless. He halted. He had emerged into a space more vast than any he had yet been in. That was obvious. About him was the atmosphere, the feeling, of sheer immensity, of empty distance.

There were no tunnel walls to guide him, he realized that another step might plunge him into a bottomless pit. Very obviously this was not the hiding place of the people he was seeking. Better retrace his steps…

A rustle out of the darkness brought him around in sudden alert, his gun ready. Looming over him, swooping down with incredible speed, was shadowy monster, giant-winged, reptile-bodied. It glowed with a pale violet radiance all its own, giving the appearance of a ghostly and very huge bat. Brand recognized it instantly, although this was his first sight of such a creature. This was the dreaded lu-bat of Luna's caves attacking him!

Desperately, he raised his steam gun, trained it on the body, depressed the trigger and held it there. The white lance leaped out, played over the luminous violet of the body, but apparently nothing was happening. The monster didn't veer in its downward course. Brand could hear the whistle of wind as it planed down at him now. He kept the steam gun pouring out its lance.

Suddenly, with devastating effect, the white lance took effect. With a tremendous roar, and a blinding flash of light, the lu-bat exploded. Brilliantly flaring fragments of it scattered and fell like meteors, or star-shells on a battlefront, into a tremendous crater.

Brand saw that he was within yards of the edge of this vast depression in the moon's inner surface. He also saw that there was apparently no other side, even in the brilliant white light that came from the flaming fragments of the lu-bat. Undoubtedly his steam gun's intensely hot ray had caused a chemical combustion in the gaseous interior of the lu-bat, releasing the radioactive elements of its make-up in flaming pyrotechnics.

But the other things that Brand saw in the brilliant light made the immensity of the depths before him inconsequential. He realized that he stood now on the rim of the famed Black Hole of Luna, the crater that had no bottom and had never been safely explored. Floating there under a ledge, concealed from above, but starkly revealed in the brilliant white light that was dying now as the lu-bat disappeared miles below still falling, was a giant space battleship. Behind it was another—and behind that a third. Brand could see no more, because darkness became complete. But registered on his dazed retina was the unmistakable identity of these super-warships. They were Martian!

Now a brilliant light bathed Brand in its rays and a voice behind him said:

"Up with the hands, Mister. And drop that gun."

Brand turned slowly, dropped his steam gun to the pumice at his feet. He tried to see beyond the bright flashlight trained on him, but couldn't.

"That's the first time I've ever seen a lu-bat knocked down with a steam gun," said the voice. "Usually it takes a heavy atom-rifle to get 'em. Never been tried with a steam gun before, as far as I know. It would be too silly to try, or would have been up to now. It seems, handled right, they do a pretty fancy job."

Brand was silent, waiting for his captor to make a move.

"Who are you?" asked the man behind the flashlight.

"Robert Wales," said Brand.

"What are you doing here?"

"Isn't that a rather silly question to ask?" Brand put in. "Judging from what I saw anchored out there…" he waved a hand in the direction of the Martian battleships he'd seen huddled against the crater wall "…I have a faint hunch my business here is of the same nature as yours."

"Judging from what you saw anchored out there," said his captor, "you haven't any business of any nature that you're going to be doing."

The man with the flashlight moved around behind Brand, and in the light, Brand saw a pathway leading toward an opening other than the one by which he had reached the Black Hole.

"Walk that way, ahead of me," directed the voice behind the flashlight. "We'll have a little business discussion with some people I know…"

Brand began moving. They moved for several hundred yards, then came to a door built into the tunnel. A guard peered forth; then the door opened.

"What you got there, Joe?" asked the guard, eyeing Brand.

"A guy I found out in the Black Hole, snooping around. He just shot down a lu-bat with a steam gun. You should have seen the fireworks. Most amazing damn thing I ever saw. Lit up the whole crater…"

"Lit it up?"

"Yeah, for miles."

"Then…"

"Sure. I'm taking him to Jeff. He's seen too much, and besides, he ain't a lu-bat hunter. No lu-bat hunter ever went after those babies with a steam gun."

"I'll say," grunted the guard. "But then, nobody ever shot one down with a steam gun either, until now." There was frank admiration in the soldier's face.

## CHAPTER SEVEN

Brand's captor ordered him ahead, and they advanced into a warm, lighted series of caverns. Down several branches, Brand saw many men, most of them in the uniform of the space-navy of Mars. His lips tightened at the sight.

"Commander Wilson," he muttered under his breath, "this isn't any sabotage, any fifth-column…it's a full-scale invasion, practically ready to go."

"What's that you said?" asked the guard sharply.

"I said this's a pretty fancy setup."

"Yea, fancier than you think…turn right, in that next room."

Brand obeyed the sudden order, entered a small room where two more guards stood, rifles in hand, rigid at attention. There was a distinct military pose to their bearing—but they were Earthmen.

Brand's captor saluted.

"Sewell, reporting to Commander Killian with a captive," he said.

Brand whirled on the man.

*"Killian!"* he exclaimed. *"Commander* Killian!"

"Of course. He's in charge here. About-face, and march in. You'll be glad to see him, no doubt, if he's an old friend of yours—and in the same business." The fellow who called himself Sewell grinned mockingly.

One of the guards opened the door, and Brand stepped through, his jaw tense, his teeth biting together so hard his jaw hurt. In his mind one raging thought flamed. Jeffry Killian was the man he sought. *Jeffry Killian was the mastermind, the arch criminal, the power behind the treachery on Luna.*

He faced the man who sat behind an ornate desk, dressed in a plain khaki uniform without insignia of any kind.

"Come to deliver your message to the *boss?"* queried Jeffry Killian softly.

"No!" said Brand savagely. "I've come to kill you! And the only thing that'll prevent me is for you to kill me first."

Jeffry Killian rose to his feet. His face was cold now.

"That can be arranged," he snapped. "I promise you that you will die, but first, I have a few things I want to talk over with you."

"Talk away!" blazed Brand, reeling under the wave of hate that was washing over him now. "I've got some talking to do myself. Some things I've been saving up to say for ten years…" He choked. "You scummy, cowardly, yellow rat!"

Killian stepped out from behind the desk, signaled covertly, and Brand found both his arms grasped by the two guards. Then Killian lashed out with a fist, flush to Brand's face.

Brand reeled under the blow. Another smashing punch sent him to his knees. He clambered back up again, eyes blazing, lips tight, but silent. At the look in his eyes, Killian stepped back, shrugged.

"That'll teach you to keep your mouth shut," he said.

He turned to Sewell.

"What's your report?"

"I found him on the edge of the Black Hole. He was attacked by a lu-bat. Shot it down with a steam gun."

"Steam-gun?"

"Yes. Kept it trained on the body, and something must've happened inside. It blew up and burned with the brightest light you ever saw. Lit up the whole crater for miles around. This gave him a good look at what we got hid out there. So I stepped in and stuck him up. He said his name was Robert Wales. Also said his business was the same as ours."

Killian laughed grimly.

"Sure it is. He's a spy, but for the other side. You can go now, Sewell. And good work. I'll see that you get a captaincy out of this."

"Thank you, sir," said Sewell, and saluting, turned and went out.

Killian eyed Brand a moment.

"Just how'd you find me?" he asked.

Brand laughed.

"By the stink."

Killian tensed, then smiled.

"Pretty crude, Boy Scout," he sneered. "About the answer I'd expect from a man of your intelligence. You never were good at anything that took any special ability outside of sheer luck. But you can bet your bottom dollar that your luck's run out now. You aren't going to get out of this with your skin. And besides, isn't that what you've always claimed you wanted? Bellyaching all over the solar system about pulling Death's tail? 'Suicide' Martin Brand. That's a laugh. And all because of a woman. How a guy with as little balance as that ever got old enough to vote, is beyond me."

Killian sat down again.

"By the way, whatever happened to Estelle?"

Brand's face went white.

"You know damn well what happened to her. You cracked her up, showing off those insane racing stunts of yours. Then when you thought you'd killed her, you thought of me, and ran like a yellow cur. Later you must have found out she'd gone insane, so you never did come back. Big enough to take a girl, but not to stay when she needed you. That's where you showed your true colors. Daredevil racer, eh? You go so fast because you're afraid of your own shadow.

"I'd never have done anything to you. If you were what Estelle wanted, that would have satisfied me. I know now it was she who sent that telegram, not you. Even you couldn't have had the colossal ego to call yourself a man, much less the best one. But at that, I guess Estelle got the kind of a man she deserved…"

Brand stopped, bit his lip. Even now the hurt of ten years ago bit deep.

Killian seemed curiously unmoved by this tirade. Instead a sneering smile played around his mouth.

Brand frowned. There was something here that he couldn't understand.

"What are you going to do with me?" he asked slowly.

"Kill you, of course," said Killian. "But not right away. I've got a few things in mind…"

"What about those ships out there?" Brand asked bluntly, waving a hand in the direction from which he'd come.

Killian laughed.

"A little hell, for Earth," he sneered. "No harm in telling you. In fact, I think I'll enjoy telling you. And when I say a 'little' hell, I mean just that. What you saw is just a sample. We've spent ten years preparing and we're just about ready. Even the Lunarians don't suspect a single thing, outside of the usual song they've been singing to deaf and dumb Earth congressmen for years, about taking the rap as buffer state between Earth and Mars in case of an *invasion*. This isn't going to be an invasion, it's going to be a picnic."

Brand's face was pale. For the first time in ten years he called upon his luck in real earnest. For the first time in ten years he *didn't* want to die.

"Just one chance…" he murmured. The almost inaudible plea was a prayer.

"What?" asked Killian sharply. "What'd you say?"

Brand stared at him, his lips tight, and said nothing.

Killian flushed. Then he rose to his feet. "Take him out, boys," he said. "Lock him up in the cell and I'll take care of him later."

The two guardsmen marched Brand between them, out of the door and down the tunnel. They took several turns, during which Brand saw many more soldiers, both Earthmen and Martian. Here and there he saw a Lunarian, also in Martian uniform. It turned his stomach. This was a hotbed of traitors, but the seriousness of it all was just beginning to strike home.

The inside of the moon was the invasion base that Commander Wilson had feared it might become. It was not a possibility, but an actual, existing, and extremely powerful base, ready for action.

Luna wouldn't be invaded from space, which was constantly watched by the Luna space fleet and the Lunarian army, but from her owns bowels—treacherously, swiftly, completely. Luna wouldn't have a chance, and Earth would then be helpless. She couldn't defend all of her great area from attack, which could be directed at any particular spot in a few hours' notice.

"Just one chance," prayed Brand. "I've got to get away!" His whisper was inaudible this time.

In a few moments the guards halted him before a barred door, opened it, thrust him inside. They locked it and one of them took up station outside, while the other returned.

Brand found himself in a rather large cave, which led back into darkness for quite some distance, and he explored it thoroughly. There was an end to it, but no other exit. His prison was indeed an effective one.

He sat down and his thoughts raced, but the more he thought, the more hopeless things became. Jeffry Killian held all the cards, and through him, Mars held a winning hand. There was no telling when the blow would fall, but it seemed certain that it would be soon.

"Got to make a break for it," he muttered. "As soon as they take me out of here...even suicide is better than letting this happen."

His face became grim. He realized that at last the luck of 'Suicide' Martin Brand had become just that...luck. Only this time it was the other kind.

Outside the prison door came the sound of a short, sharp scuffle, a heavy thudding blow, and the sound of a falling body.

Brand leaped to his feet, listening intently.

The key grated in the lock, and the door swung open. A shadowy figure entered, came toward him.

"Martin?" came the low call, melodious, haunting, familiar.

Brand froze, his blood congealed in his veins.

"Martin?" came the voice again. "Are you here? Please answer me, Martin."

Brand stumbled forward, his voice a hoarse croak of amazement, of wonder, of stunned surprise.

"Estelle!" he gasped. "Oh, my God, Estelle. It isn't..."

Now her soft hands were in his, and soft lips pressed swiftly, hurriedly, anxiously against his own.

"It is," she whispered. "I've come back to you. Thank God, Martin that I found you in time. I've been eating my heart out, wanting to tell you what a fool I've been, and how horribly sorry..."

"Estelle..." he choked out, reeling beneath the shock of it all. "You...you're all right? You aren't...?"

"No," she said softly. "I'm not...insane any more."

Her hands tugged at him.

"Come quickly," she begged. "We've got to get out of here, before Jeffry finds out..."

He allowed himself to be led out of the prison, past the unconscious body of the guard.

"Jeffry?" he mumbled. "Does he know...but how...I don't understand..."

"Never mind all that now!" pleaded Estelle Carter. "I'll explain later. Right now we've got to get away. Got to! Come...this way. I know a way out."

Her warm hand in Martin Brand's sent a strange shock to all his nerve centers. He was dazed, groping about in his mind for an explanation to this miracle that had come to him out of the dark.

"Estelle," he whispered, still unbelieving. "I don't understand..."

"Never mind," she said tensely.

"You've got to get away. Jeffry will certainly kill you."

They came to a dark opening in the basalt wall. She slipped into it and Brand followed. They groped through inky darkness for nearly a half-hour, then a hollow booming echoed out of the distance from behind them.

"The alarm," gasped Estelle. "They've discovered your escape. Oh, quickly! We've got to get out of this tunnel…"

She switched on a small flashlight and in its light, began a stumbling run down the uneven floor. Behind them, the dull booming of the alarm like a huge drum, or a bell that has cracked, throbbed incessantly. Added to it were faint shouts, hollow and eerie because of the enclosed spaces.

Suddenly, the tunnel opened on a narrow ledge, and beyond the light of the flash, Brand could see the abrupt blackness and the awful gulf that indicated the Black Hole. Out there, hanging in the darkness were those three—or more—giant Martian battleships, waiting to surge up and out into space in destructive attack on Earth.

Estelle flicked off the flashlight's beam and left them in total darkness once more. Out here the booming of the alarm shrank to almost soundless proportions, swallowed in the vastness of the emptiness around them.

"Where are we going?" Brand asked.

"There are several small cruisers from the battleships anchored along the ledge, further down. If you can reach one of them, you can escape. They'll never find you in the crater."

Brand stopped dead in his tracks. He reached out in the darkness and clutched Estelle's arm, drawing her closer to him.

"What's all this emphasis on me?" he demanded, "If I do any escaping, you're going along."

He felt, rather than saw, her head shake.

"No, Martin, please. I must stay. Nobody will know it was I who helped you escape…"

Brand gasped.

"They know you're here?"

"Yes," she said lowly. "I realize it's hard to understand, but it's too long a story to tell you now. I came here, looking for Jeffry. I remembered, even after ten years…" she hesitated and he felt her shudder "…ten years in that mad house, where to contact certain persons, and I got word to him. Then, I came…"

He stiffened and his voice grew cold.

"You came back to *him!*" he exclaimed roughly.

She stepped close, abruptly, and her warm body pressed against his and her arms went around his neck. Her breath was hot and sweet in his face.

"No!" she said fiercely. "Please, don't believe that. But he left me to die, ran away like a coward. He'll pay for that. *That's* why I came to him. He thinks I love him, but he'll know very soon that I don't."

Estelle's lips met Brand's and pressed fiercely, passionately. Almost without conscious volition, he responded, clutching her in his arms tightly, then he pushed her away.

"My God," he said hoarsely. "What's happened to you? You can't do that. You come with me. We'll get him another way. When I get back to Commander Wilson with the news I've got to tell him, there'll be action, *pronto*. We'll bottle up this invasion fleet, and smash 'em…"

She stood straight before him.

"No," she said firmly. "I'm not going with you. You can believe what you want about me. I know I treated you shamefully, and I know I deserved to lose your love. But whether or not I ever win it back again, I am going to payoff

Jeffry Killian for what he did to me. You, nor anyone else is going to stop me. Another few minutes, and they'll realize we aren't in the caves, and they'll come out here. If they find us…"

She whirled and he heard her making her way along the rocky wall. Dazed by the cold fury and deliberate intent in her voice, Brand followed, hugging the rough basalt to avoid pitching into the Black Hole's depths.

Something inside him felt like a lump of ice. It was almost a sense of fear—fear of this woman he had once loved, who had come to him now with such intense bitterness that he was appalled. Surging through him, also, was a hot emotion that he fought helplessly to thrust down. It made him speak to her now…

"Estelle…" he choked.

She stopped. His arms closed around her convulsively…

"Estelle," he said hoarsely. "Is it really you? Are you all right?"

For an instant she was still in his arms, then she spoke.

"Don't be a fool," she said coldly. "After what I did to you, are you going to let my appeal sway your reason? If, after this is all over, I can prove to you by other means that I deserve you, maybe…" her voice softened an instant, then hardened again. "How can you be so stupid as to think I might not betray you once more? Perhaps I have other motives, not good for you at all, in helping you to escape. Perhaps I intend only to do harm to Jeffry Killian by releasing you, simply because it wouldn't be a good thing for him for you to get away. I tell you, I hate him, and I intend to pay him off."

He gasped, but he had no answer to this amazing series of statements. Slowly he withdrew his arms from around her.

"Maybe you're right," he said with a curious inflection in his tone. What she had just said somehow went against his grain. It made him feel like a puppet, a helpless bystander, and placed her before him as a force that would sway him as it willed. Suddenly, he rebelled.

"Yes," he said. "Maybe you are right. Since the job I'm doing here is bigger than either of us, and certainly bigger than your personal vengeance, I'm going to take you at your word. Besides, I think my score against Killian is bigger than yours, and I say he's mine! I swore I'd get him, and I will. Show me those cruisers."

## CHAPTER EIGHT

Brand fought down the almost overpowering desire to believe what he wanted to believe about this amazingly warm and human, yet terrifyingly chilling woman before him. But they were there, those emotions, and they brought back that curious exaltation that he always felt when going into battle. Only this time it wasn't the bitter exaltation of the past ten years paced by the maddening thunder of Wagner's music. The thunder was in his blood, in a sudden uncontrollable beating of his heart. All at once he grinned in the dark...

Up from the immensity beside them shot a bright spark, leaving a trail of lesser sparks behind it that died as they drifted. Abruptly a brilliant light burst forth, and a glare filled the whole crater, lighting the walls about them with eye-blinding brilliance.

"Run!" Estelle burst out. "They've shot up a flare from the battleship!"

From the tunnel behind them came shouts, but as Brand turned, no one was in sight. They ran. Plainly revealed before them, anchored to wooden docks fastened to the sheer crater wall, were several small cruisers.

They reached them as a group of men burst from the tunnel. Estelle was ahead, and out of their sight. But they saw Brand, and a barrage of white lances leaped out at him from their steam guns. The range was too far, and they fell short.

Brand's boots rang on the planks of the dock, and he ran toward Estelle. He reached out for her.

"Now," he panted. "You're getting in with me and we're off…"

She slipped out of his grasp. In her hand appeared a tiny steam gun.

"No," she said coldly. "Get in and go."

He eyed her a second.

"You won't shoot," he decided with a grin. He leaped forward…

A lance of white leaped out, and the planks at his feet curled and crackled in flame and splinters. Amazed, he lurched to a halt, drew back.

*"Get in!"* she screamed. *"Before it's too late!"*

The shouts of the men from the tunnel were close now. Brand hesitated one single furious second, then plunged into one of the cruisers and slammed the cowl shut. Out of the corner of his eye he saw her leap into another.

But he had no time to be surprised at this new maneuver. He shot the cruiser into the emptiness beyond the dock. Lances from steam guns were piercing the darkness around the cruiser now, while above the flare faded and died. Behind him, the cruiser piloted by Estelle bore at him. Its bow gun flamed fire, and a blast of energy seared past him.

*"Damn,"* he swore in shock and surprised anger. *She was shooting at him!*

With wild rage in his heart, he slammed the throttle down to the floor, and whipped the tiny cruiser into the black depths beyond the great battleship and in an instant he was lost in pitch blackness that was broken only by the faint flash of steam guns far behind on the ledge. He had gotten away, clean.

Burning anger seethed through him as he set the automatic black-light pilot in operation. That would prevent him from crashing against a crater wall, even though it was hundreds of miles to the other side. As the cruiser rushed on in the blackness, his thoughts calmed. With curious certainty, he realized that the blast from Estelle's bow guns had been deliberately close, yet far enough harmlessly to miss him. He realized that if Estelle had wished, she could have blasted him completely. She had missed intentionally.

And now, she was back there, probably docking again, to report failure in stopping him. Then she'd carry out the cold words she had spoken to him, return to Jeffry Killian to carry her vengeance to the chilling conclusion that Martin Brand knew suddenly she would. In spite of the memory of her loveliness, the recollection of the soft warmth and allure of her body, Brand shuddered.

"My God," he whispered. "What's happened to her?"

Brand turned off the motors of the cruiser and drifted silently along in the utter blackness of the Black Hole. Vainly his eyes tried to pierce the gloom, tried to see either a light indicating an exit to the surface, or a distant rock wall that might glow with phosphorescence and allow him to follow it to an opening back into Luna's interior.

Right now he was somewhere in Luna's crust, which ranged from five hundred to a mere two hundred miles in thickness. A sense of dizziness swept over him momentarily as he discovered that he couldn't determine which was up and which was down. In fact, he floated aimlessly in emptiness so complete that he had absolutely no sense of direction, if such a thing as direction had ever existed.

Suddenly he knew the reason for the legends and terror attached to being lost in the famed Black Hole—for he realized now that he was lost. Out in empty space, no matter how vast it seemed, there were always stars—millions of them, all recognizable in their formations, so that direction was merely a matter of a star map. Here, in utter blackness, space lost its immensity, and became a black shell that pressed hard against one. Beyond it was nothing—not even in imagination.

In spite of himself, an eerie sensation of terror crept over Brand. His hands remained calm, and his thoughts crept deliberately over his problem, but the hair on his neck rose in unexplained terror. The Black Hole was demonstrating its most terrible feature—its ability to immerse those lost within its immensities in terrifying mind-chilling panic.

"Steady, Martin," he told himself. "The wall of this thing is right behind you, back where the docks are."

Even as his voice sounded muffled in the cockpit of the tiny cruiser, Brand knew that "behind" was just another word. He didn't know which direction *had been* behind. Now it was just the other way from ahead.

He shot back the cowl of the cruiser, and breathed the heady atmosphere of Luna's interior. It seemed curiously rare here, and he grinned suddenly.

"That's it!" he exclaimed.

For a moment he drove the ship at high speed, having once more closed the cowl, then he shut off the motor, opened the cowl, and breathed deeply. The air was rarer than before.

"Up!" he said exultantly. "Who's lost!"

Carefully he noted the calibrations on the meters on the control board, then swung the ship around in a one hundred-eighty degree arc. Again he opened up the motor and blasted through the blackness.

A half-hour later the motor-jets ceased firing.

The enormity of the catastrophe that had happened dawned on him with a rush. The cruiser still hurtled along at high speed, but it would gradually slow down, then it would drift toward the nearest crater wall and land there. From then on it would be a matter of making his way on foot.

On foot. In the Black Hole.

He looked hopefully at the fuel indicator, pounded it with his fist, but the needle remained stationary—at the empty mark.

"I hope they're as careless with those battleships," he growled angrily.

He settled back in the seat, helpless to do any thing but scowl at the dimly illuminated instrument panel. He took mental stock of his situation. He had no weapons on his person, but he did have a gun mounted in the bow, which was too heavy to detach and carry.

He fumbled about the interior of the cruiser, but it was tiny, and obviously never intended for fighting purposes. There were no other weapons. Furthermore, there was no food, nor water.

He had no flashlight, and to walk *anywhere* in this giant crater without a light would be a suicidal undertaking.

For several hours he drifted aimlessly, fretting at the inaction. His speed, according to the indicator, had dropped to a mere eight miles per hour. He might drift endlessly at that rate, depending on his direction in relation to the walls of the Black Hole.

As he debated on this possibility, he was hurled forward in his seat as the cruiser crashed into solid rock. Even at this slow speed, the shock was abrupt, although not enough to injure him. After the noise of the crash was gone, the silence enveloped him. The lights on the cruiser had gone out. The only indication of life was his own breathing, which boomed loudly in his own ears.

Brand leaned forward in the darkness, fumbled at the instrument panel. He swore vehemently several times, but finally he came up with a dashlight, which he'd wrested whole from the panel. With it came a handful of wire torn from its bowels, and several batteries.

It took fully fifteen minutes to connect them up, and the result was a dim glow that spread radiance only a few feet in each direction. It was enough of a glow for him to see that he had crashed on a barren rock surface. Judging from the weight of his body, which was about twenty-five moon pounds, he was at the moment perched precariously on the steep perpendicular wall of the Black Hole. In relation to the moon itself, he was actually standing at right angles to the perpendicular. Gravity was a peculiar thing on this hollow world.

Then he climbed out of the cruiser and walked to its bow. He considered it a moment then began walking slowly forward in the direction the bow indicated he had been traveling when the cruiser had struck. That way would be "down" toward the interior of the moon. To walk was a difficult task as due to the light gravity, he often found himself twisting helplessly in the air.

Behind him, in the darkness, Brand heard a faint rustling, a swish of moving air, and he turned awkwardly. There was a rushing sound, growing in the dark like the nearing approach of some huge body, and the skin crawled on his scalp. The dim light he carried only served to accentuate the darkness beyond its range, and he could see nothing.

In desperation he tore the wires loose from their connections, and the light went out. As he did so, the cause of the rushing wind became obvious. Swooping down, almost upon him, was the dreaded, faintly glowing body of a lu-bat.

Before he could dodge its attack, a curiously light but strong body crashed into him, and cruel talons dug into his flesh. A pair of powerful tentacles wrapped themselves around him, and with a dizzying rush he felt himself carried aloft at terrific speed.

For a moment, the pain of the talons clutching him and the shock of the attack had dazed him, but when he recovered his senses, he realized that he was being carried to some unknown destination at express-train pace. He had no doubt as to what this destination was—the nest of the lu-bat. The purpose—food for young lu-bats!

He became aware that he still clutched the wires from his makeshift light in his hand, but the light itself and the batteries were gone. He was about to drop the wire also, when a thought struck him. He had a grim look of determination as he squirmed around and peered up at the scrawny neck of the lu-bat, which was bobbing up and down as it flew through the increasingly heavy Lunarian atmosphere.

"You'll never get me to that nest," he vowed softly. "Because where I go, corpse or not, you'll go too."

With a painful effort, he slung the loose end of the wire around the lu-bat's neck, and tied a secure, but loosely looped, knot in it. Then he removed the empty steam gun holster from his belt, inserted it in the coil of the wire, and twisted it slowly until it began to tighten around the neck of the Lu-bat like a tourniquet.

Then, hands on the holster, he waited. If he killed the creature now it would mean dashing himself to death when they crashed to the surface. If he waited, he could apply the pressure, and it would be a battle to the death. If he won...

His jaw tightened.

"The luck of 'Suicide' Martin Brand will have to be better than it ever has before," he whispered softly to himself.

The giddy swaying of the lu-bat's motion was beginning to make Brand very sick, and the pain of the creature's talons was becoming intense. He could feel blood running down one side, as the cruel claws pierced his skin. He used one hand to tear at the tentacles holding him, and they tightened, but the talons loosened, releasing him altogether as the lu-bat became aware of his efforts and concentrated on wrapping him more tightly in the tentacles.

Brand gasped for breath and desisted his efforts. If this was any indication, the lu-bat was going to have all the better of the strangling contest which would begin the moment he tightened that tourniquet.

Below his feet, Brand saw a faint glowing spot, and he peered intently. The rush of wind in his eyes prevented accurate observation, but suddenly he identified it.

"A city!" he exclaimed.

The tentacles around his body tightened convulsively. His explosive utterance had alarmed the lu-bat. Blackness washed over his vision in a wave that was not the blackness of the Black Hole.

When he could see again, the dim spot of light was gone. It was only when he relocated it off to the side a few minutes later that he realized the lu-bat had changed its course. All at once Brand noticed a difference in the darkness. There was sharp line where pitch black ended and a slightly lesser degree of black began.

The edge of the Black Hole.

He was *out* of the "pit of lost men." He was being carried by the bat through the atmosphere of inner Luna itself.

Then he noticed that the black rim was sliding upward a bit, and coming nearer. The lu-bat wasn't emerging from the pit, but merely heading toward what was possibly its lair somewhere along the inner edge of that rim. As they drew nearer, Brand tightened his grip on the steam gun holster, and readied himself for a quick series of twists that would tighten the innocuous, but deadly strand of wire around the beast's throat.

The lu-bat slackened speed and hovered an instant over a ledge. Brand saw the darker opening of a small cave that slid smoothly downward. This was undoubtedly the bat's lair, and perhaps an impossible place out of which to climb. In quick determination, Brand twisted frantically on the tourniquet. It was now or never!

The wire loop sank out of sight into the leathery neck of the lu-bat, and a fearsome squawk became a screaming gurgle. Instantly, Brand found himself the center of a cyclone of pain and swirling action.

The tentacles tightened convulsively around him, and he felt a rib crack with agonizing torture. His head seemed to be swelling and about to burst. The air rushed out of his lungs as though he were being smashed beneath a steamroller. The talons of the lu-bat sank into his shoulder and cut deeply.

Almost in a faint, Brand continued to twist, then stopped, conscious despite the whirlwind of tossing and floundering around, that too much twisting might snap the wire and allow the pressure to be released.

He hung on, managed to slip one end of the holster beneath the loop of the knot in the wire itself. This, he did so it wouldn't spin around and loosen the tourniquet when unconsciousness would cause him to lose his grip.

He felt the huge beast smash into the ground…one leg went numb with the blow. One hand was torn from his grip on the holster, and ground against a rocky surface that shredded his skin.

Tremendous shocks buffeted him as the lu-bat flopped around. Then he felt himself hurled fifty feet through the air, and despite the low gravity, he landed with a stunning, bone-breaking crash at the base of the wall that marked the inner edge of the ledge. He felt his body slipping slowly over the edge of the lu-bat's nest, and glimpsed below him the yawning mouths and the staring eyes of a dozen small lu-bats, who were lunging about in excitement and anticipation of the feast that awaited them.

Frantically, with his last conscious effort, Brand clawed his fingers into the creviced rock and tried to drag his body back from its precarious position. The tremendous thrashing of the dying parent lu-bat raised a din in his ears that kept him from the brink of unconsciousness for the moment, but then he found himself going limp, and his fingers released their grip. He slipped down…

A tremendous blow from the lu-bat's wing smashed into him, and the lu-bat flopped down past him into its lair. Brand was almost unaware of the tremendous commotion that resulted below him as all went black and sound was blotted out by terrible silence.

## CHAPTER NINE

Martin Brand found himself lying in a bed and suddenly became aware of his surroundings in a very unsatisfactory manner to him. He discovered that it was distinctly no pleasure to awake and find every limb aching and his head feeling as though a dozen imps were pounding on his skull with red-hot hammers.

But there was one thing that was certainly not painful. Instead, it was strangely soft, cool and caressing. It ran soothingly across his forehead in a gentle way that reminded him of a woman's fingers…woman's fingers?

Looking down into his eyes were the cool blue ones of the mystery girl, the girl who had killed a man to save his life—for no reason at all.

He closed his eyes.

"No," he whispered to himself. "I'm lying in a hole with baby lu-bats picking my bones clean. I can't be in a bed, with *her* nursing me. It just isn't logical."

"But it's true," came her calm voice, soft and melodious. "You are in bed. I *am* stroking your forehead, and the lu-bats *aren't* picking your bones…because I got to you before you fell to them."

He opened his eyes again.

"The luck of Suici…" he shut his lips tightly, suddenly. Then he went on, covering up his 'near' slip. "The luck of Satan himself must be with me."

"Yes, Martin Brand," she said, "your luck is still holding out. No need to look startled, or alarmed. I know who you are, and why you are here."

Brand lifted himself on one elbow and groaned. "Damn!" he said feelingly. "I'm all busted up."

He sank back again, and continued what he had been about to say.

"You know an awful lot, too much, in fact. Just who are you, anyway."

"My name," she said, "is Kathleen Dennis. My number is 28, and my sector is 24A, Luna. You have two broken ribs. We are in my ship somewhere near the Liebnitz mountains and a small crater near the Black Hole. And you are going to stay right where you are until you are able to get back to work."

He stared at her.

"That's just dandy. And who says so?"

"Special Services."

"Do you mean to tell me," he asked wonderingly, "that you, a woman, are in the Special Service working on the same problem I am?"

She nodded.

"Is that so unusual? Don't you think I can handle the job?"

"So far," he said wryly. "I'm in no position to deny that. And I'm rather relieved to know you killed Ormandy because he had me on the spot. I had you ticketed for a different set-up..." he stopped and his eyes narrowed slightly, "...maybe it is a different set-up!"

"You mean you don't believe my story?"

He looked at her steadily.

"Personally, I'd like to, but actually, I'd be a fool to. You may be one of the gang. Just the same, your orders don't go with me. I'm getting up right now, and doing a little sending over your radio."

Brand tossed back the covers, grimacing with the pains his motions caused, and tired to get his feet (which he discovered were bare) out onto the floor. He was clad in brilliant blue pajamas, certainly not at all intended for the male sex.

"You've certainly taken some liberties," he said with some confusion, "or is the orderly out on an errand?"

"There is no orderly," she said, "and you aren't getting up, nor are you sending anything over any radio." She put her hands gently on his shoulders and pressed him back on the pillows.

"Oh, yes, I am," he said angrily. "It's a matter of vital importance. And if you don't let me get up, I'll fix you, but good."

She crossed the tiny cabin, took his clothes from a locker, and walked to the door.

"You can have these," she said, "after you feel better. As for your 'vital' message, I've already taken care of that. I radioed the home base of the presence of armed enemy ships in the Black Hole. He is sending in a patrol cruiser in a few hours."

"A patrol cruiser!" gasped Brand, sitting up in spite of the pain. "Good God, girl, that crater is full of *battleships!* The minute a cruiser shows up, it'll be blasted wide open. It'll never come back out of the Black Hole."

She looked at him curiously.

"Do you really believe that?" she asked. "I told headquarters base you were babbling about battleships, but he was convinced you were delirious. Such ships could not possibly have gotten into Luna. They'd have to pass the fleet, and they could not have come down the entrance crater on Dark Side. There is no other crater through which they could enter."

"What about the one you just told me about?" he asked. "If you came out near the Liebnitz range from a crater that opens near the Black Hole, the answer is obvious."

She smiled sweetly.

"Too small," she said. "It's known only to the Special Service, and it's through that the patrol ship will go with barely enough room. That's the main reason a patrol is being sent. The other is simply to check on your belief, however wrong, that there are armed forces in the Black Hole."

She moved into the doorway.

"Where are you going with my clothes?" he demanded, scrambling painfully half out of bed.

"Somewhere where you won't be tempted to put them on and leave this ship," she said. "And too, I have work to do. I have to guide the patrol to the crater entrance. They don't know where it is."

She shut the door, and as he stared, he heard the lock turn.

"Damn," he said loudly.

With a groan, he heaved himself erect, crossed to the door and rattled the knob.

"You crazy little fool!" he shouted. "That patrol ship will never come out. Let me out of here! I'll radio Commander Wilson myself."

There was no answer, and as he stood there, the ship lurched, and took off slowly. He reeled back to the bunk, sat down, and hung on until the ship leveled off. Then he got up again, crossed to the lockers and opened each one in turn. The first was bare; the other held a regulation space suit. He grunted, then with great effort, he climbed into it. When he had completed his job of makeshift clothing, he removed the small crowbar from the belt of the space suit. He crossed to the door and inserted it between door and jamb. Then, sweating with the pain the effort caused, he pressed until the lock sprang open and the door swung inward.

He gripped the steam gun from the holster in the space suit and walked unsteadily down the tiny corridor toward the control room. Here he found the girl seated at the controls. She was looking out of the observation window. There was another ship out there, a patrol cruiser. Brand recognized its sleek lines.

He stood behind the girl, leveled his gun.

"Okay, Kathleen," he said, his voice muffled in the space suit, "you can open up the radio key and send a little message to that patrol."

She whirled around, faced him.

She took one amazed glance at the space suit, then she smiled.

"I forgot the suit," she confessed.

"I'd have come in the pajamas," he said grimly, "or without, if necessary. That patrol has got to stop."

Her eyes narrowed.

"Why?"

"Because it's suicide," he said angrily. He opened the face plate on the suit.

"Open that key," he demanded. "I'm in no mood to fool around."

She turned and pressed the key.

Then she spoke into the transmitter. "Twenty-eight calling Space Patrol N-twenty-seven."

The reply came instantly.

"Space Patrol N-twenty-seven. Ready for message."

Brand leaned over, grasped the microphone in his free hand.

"Cancel that order to investigate," he said. "It's suicide. There are at least three heavy battle cruisers anchored inside, and they'll blast you to atoms in two seconds."

"What..." came a startled gasp from the patrol ship. "Battle cruisers...hey, wait a minute. I'll have to call Captain Craig." There was a moment's pause, then the voice of the operator came in again.

"Who are you?" asked the puzzled voice. "Is this the ship alongside?"

"Yes," said the girl. "I'm right here. At the moment I have a steam gun in my back. My patient has refused to believe I have orders from headquarters."

"I believe 'em," snapped Brand. "That's what's bothering me. I know what you fellows are going into, and I've got to stop it."

A new voice cut in.

"Captain Craig calling," the voice said. "What's the trouble, twenty-eight?"

"Captain," said Brand urgently. "This is Martin Brand. I've discovered at least three of Mars' biggest battleships anchored in the Black Hole. If you go in there, you'll be blasted out of existence..."

"What did you say your name was?" asked Captain Craig's voice with a peculiar note to it.

"Martin Brand," snapped Brand. "I am a Special Service operative, acting under Commander Wilson."

"Commander Wilson, eh? Whoever you are," said the radio, "land at once and prepare for boarding..." The radio went dead.

Brand stared down at Kathleen in surprise. Her hand was on the key.

"What'd you do that for?" he asked. "And what does he mean 'whoever I am'?"

Her face was white, and there was something in her eyes akin to terror.

"Martin," she said tensely. "Commander Wilson died four days ago of a heart attack. So, when Captain Craig questioned your identity, he had good reason. Another thing: Didn't you know that a public funeral was held for you when you became Robert Wales in actuality a week ago? Commander Wilson deemed it the wisest course, because he knew things were about to break. So when you said Martin Brand..."

Brand's senses whirled dizzily around him.

"You mean...?" he gasped.

"Yes. I lied to you when I said I radioed about the battleships. I did radio, but could only report suspicious activity in this locality. If this Special Service thing were to become known to the Senate..."

"Then Craig intends to arrest me?" questioned Brand harshly.

"Yes. And when he does, he'll arrest you as Robert Wales. You'll be exiled to Venus, perhaps, but that's better than being shot as a spy..."

Kathleen's voice was trembling strangely.

"I only wanted to save you from the terrible situation you are in..."

A moment Brand stared at her curiously. Then he smiled.

"I'm not in a jam," he said. "Commander Wilson foresaw that something might happen to him, so he placed a complete record on file, to be opened in an emergency concerning Robert Wales, which will completely exonerate me and reveal me as a Special Service agent. It will even prove that my original conviction, under the name of Robert Wales, was a put-up job to conceal my true mission, and give me access to the plots and counterplots of the fifth-columnists."

Kathleen rose to her feet and faced him, her face even whiter than before. "No, Martin," she said, "you are wrong. There are no such papers. A week ago the Bureau of Records of the Special Service was completely wrecked by an explosion, and every document was burned in the resulting fire. I am the only other living being who knows you are Martin Brand, and I couldn't prove it. I can't even prove you are Robert Wales..."

For a long moment Brand stared at her in stunned surprise. Then, the tiny cruiser rocked as a shell exploded across her bow.

"We've got to land!" Kathleen cried. "They're shooting a warning over our bow!"

Abruptly Brand pushed her aside, slid into the control seat, ignoring the agony in his chest.

"Where's that crater opening?" he asked savagely. "Straight ahead?"

"Yes," she said. *"No, we're over it now!"* Her eyes were fixed on the observation window. "But Martin, please don't, they'll shoot us down..."

Below them Martin Brand saw the small, dark opening of the crater. With a motion that hurled the girl into a corner in a heap, and pressed him savagely back into his seat with pain grinding in his chest, he sent the cruiser hurtling down into the black depths. The brilliance of sunlight was replaced by pitch darkness. It was lighted momentarily by the brilliant flash of a magnesium-atomic exploding against the wall beyond him as the patrol ship took a desperate shot at him in a crippling attempt. The light showed Brand what he needed, and for the next six seconds he drove the cruiser down a narrow, slanting shaft with death at each elbow. Then and only then did he turn on the lights.

A scream came from behind him.

*"Martin! We're going to crash…! This tunnel turns at right angles two miles down."*

Looming up a mile ahead was the wall of rock that seemed to be the end of the tunnel. Rockets roared and flame filled the crater shaft as Martin gave the decelerators everything the ship had. Blackness reeled in on him, but he hung on grimly, ignoring the pain in his chest that threatened to engulf him in unconsciousness.

Even through the walls of the ship the scream of the bow rockets was audible…and it was the last thing Brand heard before he sighed helplessly and eased down into a feathery oblivion—that and his own tortured voice whispering in agony: "Damn those broken ribs…"

It was a dream. It couldn't be anything else…waking in a bed, feeling a cool hand on his forehead, opening his eyes to stare up into the deep blue ones of the girl with the red hair—that had all happened before.

"How do you feel now?" Kathleen asked.

He looked up at her, and puckered his brows.

"I feel pretty good," he admitted. "But all this is a little cockeyed. It's happened before, and that isn't logical. This time I'm only dreaming. I'll wake up, and find myself lying in the bottom of a crater…"

He sat up, discovered that his ribs were still sore, but was conscious that all the agonizing pain was gone.

"Hey! I *am* awake! And this isn't…a ship. It's…"

"It's a hospital in Luna City," said Kathleen. "I flew you here after ducking the patrol in the crater shaft. They went on to the Black Hole to investigate. I found some papers in your clothes saying you were Edgar Barnes, prospector, and I told them I'd picked you up after you had been attacked by lu-bats."

"How long ago was that?" asked Brand urgently.

"Oh, I brought you here over a week ago. You've been in a pretty bad way."

"I don't mean that!" exploded Brand impatiently. "How long ago since the patrol ship went into the Black Hole?"

"They went in immediately after we eluded them. But no one in Luna knows it."

"Any report since?"

"I don't know. I had to hide my ship in a crater. Besides, the radio got smashed when we hit the wall…"

"Hit the wall?"

"Yes, but not hard. You had the ship nearly stopped when we reached the turn in the crater shaft."

"You took over from there, hid from the patrol, and took me here, concealing my identity?"

"Yes."

"Do you know what you've done? You've aided a criminal to escape. You've placed yourself in a situation as impossible to explain as my own. I'm a nobody now. I'm dead and buried. Even my mock-personality is non-existent. I am an assumed name, which can't hold up a minute under inspection, with the strange angle that when the fraud is discovered, there's no real name to tack onto me. I'm the living example of a nonentity!"

"Yes," she said. "I know what I've done."

"Why are you doing it?" he asked bluntly.

She looked at him a long moment, then she spoke slowly.

"First, because it's part of my work. I have a job to do, which is just as necessary for me to carry through, as yours is for you. Now, with the situation the way it is, the whole thing is left up to me. The second and I guess, the best explanation is because I love you."

Brand sat bolt upright in bed. "What!"

Her eyes met his steadily.

"For ten years I've admired you—no, longer. I think I loved you, in a worshiping, little-girl way even before your intended marriage. I was happy when I thought you had found your happiness, and I cried when she jilted you. I've cried many times since then—every time I heard another story of 'Suicide' Martin Brand and his reckless exploits on the space lanes. Everybody called you a lucky fool, a fighting daredevil who always seemed to bear a charmed life, who always won what he fought for. But I knew the real drive behind you. I knew the unhappiness that filled you, the hurt you were trying to hide, the ache you were trying to kill, and the memories you were trying to forget.

"I joined the Service simply because I loved you, and I wanted to find you, and follow you, and meet you...and try to take the place of that, that..."

She paused and her eyes fell finally. But she went on:

"Once I almost met you. It was in a bar. You were too drunk to notice anybody, and I was sitting nearby. I heard you say something that proved all I knew about what really goes on inside you. You said, to no one in particular, because you were alone: 'I wanted a woman, a woman who could ride the stars with me in a little cottage on the seashore…' When you said that, Martin, I discovered I wanted to be that woman…"

Her voice ceased, and her eyes lifted again, looked at his.

For a long moment there was silence while he looked at her, while he fought for something to say. Then it was she who spoke.

"I know I'm making a fool out of myself, but what I've said had to be said now, because I think it will be the last chance I will ever have to say it. I'm going now, and I won't see you again. You had better go too. Your work is ended. You must leave here, because even if no one on Earth will believe who you are, there are people here who know, and they will see that you are removed."

"You crazy little fool," said Brand chokingly. "You crazy little fool. Somebody ought to spank you." He swung his legs out of the bed and stood up. "Call an orderly. I want my clothes. I'm getting out of here right now, and I'm damned if I'm going to run away. Commander Wilson is still my boss, and he gave me a job to do. I'm going to do it, if I can."

She stood staring at him.

"Please," she pleaded. "You must go away. You can't do anything. Even if you found out the truth, you couldn't make any Earth official believe it…"

"Then I'll do it myself," said Brand. "I *know* the truth." That Black Hole is filled with Martian battleships, and they'll be coming out soon to blast at Earth. Then it'll be too late. And why you, who are supposed to be on the same mission I am, keep insisting on letting that happen, I can't understand. If you say you know me so well, and are in love with me, which is the wildest thing I ever heard of, then why don't you help me, instead of hindering me?"

Her face burned red. Then she spoke, and her voice was level.

"I'll send an orderly. Put your clothes on and meet me in the lobby. We're going to the Black Hole...*together.* And if you can show me those battleships..."

She whirled and almost ran from the room while Brand stared after her in amazement and bewilderment.

## CHAPTER TEN

In a few minutes the orderly came, and Brand asked for his clothes.

"I'm leaving," he said. "Please have my bill made out..."

"It's been paid," said the orderly.

Brand flushed.

"Then get my clothes," he barked. "I'm in a hurry."

Ten minutes later he walked down the hallway, rather unsteadily, but with growing strength as he regained a surety of step. He went down in the elevator, walked into the lobby. He glanced around, but saw no one.

Suddenly he noticed two men advancing toward him. One was dressed in the uniform of the Lunar Police. The other was the taxi-driver Brand had marooned in the crater-bottom near the Black Hole.

"You're under arrest," said the Lunarian officer.

Brand's eyes narrowed and he tensed himself. He eyed the taxi-driver who now was dressed in civilian clothes and stood looking at him with a strange calmness in his manner, a peculiar glint in his eyes.

"What for?" asked Brand.

"For theft, for attack with intent to do great bodily harm, for kidnapping, and if that isn't enough...for murder," said the officer. "Put out your hands."

There was a pair of handcuffs in one hand, and a steam gun in his other. It was leveled straight at Brand's heart.

As Brand put out his hands reluctantly, there came a slight hissing. The light globe in the ceiling shattered, and the room was plunged into darkness. Brand hurled himself instantly to one side. A brilliant lance of white pierced the spot where his body had been. Brand stumbled over a chair, picked it up and hurled it savagely at the spot where the officer had been standing. There was a thud, a muffled curse, and the sound of a falling body, but Brand wasn't waiting to hear more. He plunged toward the door, which was dimly lighted from the street lights outside.

Without bothering to open it, he shielded his head in his arms and hurled his body straight through the thin plastic-glass. It shattered with a crash, and he fell to the sidewalk outside. Parked at the curb was a taxi, which Brand hurled himself into. With one savage blow he knocked the driver unconscious, then dumped him over the side.

From somewhere down the street a white flash came. The glass of the windshield shattered and frosted weirdly under the effect of the intensely hot steam bolt from a steam gun. But Brand had the taxi under way now, and it hummed into the air, flashed around the corner of a building, and roared upward into the darkness of inner Luna.

Behind him a fast ship, not a cab, was climbing in pursuit. Brand realized it was a police flier, obviously the vehicle of the officer who had come in to arrest him, with a fellow officer in it. Apparently the encounter with Brand on his feet, when they had expected to arrest him in his bed, had caught them a bit unaware.

The ship behind was by far faster than the cab, but Brand had gotten a good start. Now, against the pitch black of the inner world's eternal midnight sky, Brand knew it would be a difficult job for them to spot him. He made sure every light was out, then sent the cab hurtling on a tangent. Three times he changed directions, then zoomed down close to the rocky surface and slowed so that his motor roar became a dull humming. He searched the black vault above him with keen eyes.

The pursuing ship was nowhere in sight.

"Those Lunar police are no fools," he said. "They've probably doused their lights too, and are waiting for me to come up again."

Brand studied the faint lighted spots that indicated Lunar cities far above on the other side of the hollow ball and tried to determine his whereabouts. Finally he nodded grimly, then sent the taxi humming toward the north of Lunar City. If he hadn't forgotten, it was near there he would find a familiar crater...

A half-hour later he was sure his directions were right. He rose higher in the air, and increased his speed. Ahead loomed the black spot that was the crater. Abruptly a brilliant beam of light bathed the ship in its rays. Behind him the police ship bore down on him.

"Right," gasped Brand. "He *wasn't* so dumb. That guy's a real policeman!"

There was admiration in his voice, even as he shot the taxi down at the limit of its speed, straight for the edge of the crater. He looped over it fast, dropped down like a plummet. Then he leveled off and landed on the now familiar ledge. He whirled the wheel of the cab, faced it on an angle toward the farther edge of the crater, stepped out, and shot the motor button all the way down. He dropped to the ledge in a heap as the taxi roared upward and away. It raced out of the crater like a meteor, its exhausts visible now with the tremendous speed.

He dropped behind a boulder and waited. The police ship roared over the edge of the crater, spun violently to avoid collision, then looped to follow the hurtling, driverless taxi. Both ships bore away on a straight line at tremendous speed, and Brand, chuckled.

"He thought I intended to drive him against the wall with that maneuver. Now he'll follow until he gets me."

From behind Brand there came a shout, and he turned to see armed men pouring from the tunnel at the base of the ledge. They had seen him land, and were after him.

Brand rose to his feet, ran back into the shadows along the crater wall and raced along. Around him bolts from steam guns were hitting. He ducked low, unable to fire back. He had no steam gun this time. It hadn't been with his clothes. A sudden memory staggered him in his stride and he stopped in his tracks, retraced his steps several yards, anxiously scanned the base of the crater wall where it met the floor of the ledge. His pursuers, amazed at this inexplicable maneuver, slowed down, several dropped behind boulders.

Then Brand saw it…the atomic rifle he had taken from the Martian guard he'd killed the first time he landed on this ledge.

He seized it, dropped flat on his stomach, and sighted at the advancing men. Brilliant explosions rocked the ledge. Several men went down like stricken sheep. Brand fired quickly, methodically, and in a moment the ledge before him seemed deserted. All of his attackers who had not been killed, had hidden themselves as effectively as possible.

Brand laid down a thundering barrage of shots that blanked out the ledge in waves of smoke and dust, then he leaped to his feet and ran back the way he had originally been heading. In the black shadows he almost ran into the aero-taxi where he had hidden it. With a thrill of thankfulness he climbed into it, slid into the driver's seat, and sent the craft humming into the darkness of the crater, hidden from view of the men on the ledge by the smoke that still hung thickly around the scene of the exploded atomic shells.

A moment later he was over the edge and speeding forward toward the Black Hole.

"Now to find out about that patrol ship," he said grimly.

It was obvious that the system of caves through which he had traveled originally to reach the Black Hole was located between the crater he had just left, and the Black Hole itself. Therefore, the Martians would be anchored directly below him and perhaps only four or five miles down.

That hunch proved to be correct. As Brand allowed his aero-cab to drift slowly down in the inky blackness, the bulk of a tremendous vessel loomed up suddenly, so close that he grazed the giant hull.

Brand stopped the cab short, hung motionless under the belly of the great, deadly fish of space. He could see its bulk dimly, stretching for a thousand yards in each direction. Somewhere off to his left would be the wooden docks where the small cruisers were located. If properly fueled, one of those ships would be much better than the unarmed aero-cab. Against the giant battleships, they would be as impotent as a mosquito, of course, but Brand had no intention of attempting anything so futile.

He moved the aero-cab slowly along under the belly of the monster ship, noting the huge bomb racks with their gaping openings. Those bombs were hydrogen atomic bombs, just as were the bullets in his atomic rifle. They must never be loosed on Earth!

He sent the aero-cab toward the wooden docks, and reached them in pitch darkness. With some unavoidable bumping around, he managed to make the cab fast and climbed onto the dock. He couldn't see whether there were any cruisers tied up there or not.

"Can't risk a light," he muttered.

He dropped to his hands and knees and crawled along the docks, so as not to stumble off into space. At each mooring post, he felt for a cable that would indicate a cruiser moored there.

Finally he found one. The gangplank was down, and in a moment he had opened the lock and stepped inside. This ship was considerably larger than the one he had escaped in before. It was at least a ten-man cruiser, and when he had closed the lock, he fumbled for the light switch and snapped it on.

Lying on the floor at his feet was the body of a Martian guard, his face seared away by a steam gun blast and his body lying in a pool of blood.

"My God!" exclaimed Brand in stunned surprise, unable to fathom the meaning of this discovery.

Swiftly Brand snapped off the lights and stood still. Was there anybody else on this ship? He listened intently, but heard no sound. Softly he made his way forward. This cruiser would have a radio—and it was the radio he wanted to find. He reached the control room door and opened it softly. It was dark inside. He closed the door behind him, then groped forward.

Behind him a flashlight beam lanced out, caught him full in the back. His own shadow loomed gigantically against the control board ahead of him.

"Don't move," said a chill feminine voice. "Raise your arms into the air slowly."

"Estelle!" he gasped, and whirled around.

"Martin!" For an instant the voice held unutterable shock, and she stood as though paralyzed. He couldn't see her face distinctly behind the brightness of the flashlight, but for an infinitesimal fraction of a second, he thought he saw annoyance mirrored in her tight lips.

Then abruptly she snapped out the flashlight and was in his arms, her lips pressed against his passionately, devouringly. She was sobbing.

"Oh Martin, Martin, I'm so glad you've come back. I'm in terrible trouble…"

Brand stood there, holding her in his arms tightly, a strange tumult in his breast.

"Estelle…" he choked. "I…"

The soft shaking of her shoulders and hungry pressure of her lips stirred him as nothing had ever stirred him before. But even in the confusion of it all, he remembered the near-miss of her guns as she had tried to shoot him down as he escaped into the Black Hole.

She must have sensed the doubt in his half-yielding lips, and reading his mind, she said, "You thought I was shooting at you?" she questioned tearfully. "I *wasn't*, Martin. I only wanted to make it look as though I was trying to get you. So that Jeffry Killian would trust me when I came back to him…"

His hands were on her shoulders, holding her at arm's length.

"Came back?" he asked. "You mean you wanted him to believe you were a friend, and your real intention was revenge?"

"Yes," she said slowly. "I hate him…more than I love you, if that's possible. I wanted to kill him; torture him slowly first, then kill him just as slowly. But I…" she paused.

Brand tried to see her features in the dark and failed.

"What did you say?" he whispered hoarsely.

"I wanted to kill him…" she began.

"No, no. You said something else…"

She lifted his hands from her shoulders, pressed close to him, and…this time her lips kissed his cheeks, his lips, his nose, and finally buried themselves at his neck.

"I said 'as much as I love you'," she whispered. "And I *do,* Martin. Oh, I do, so very much…"

A fiery exaltation was suddenly surging through Brand's veins, and there was exultation in his voice.

"Thank God, Estelle, I've gotten you back at last. I've been going mad for ten years, with hunger for you, with memories…"

He kissed her lips tenderly, then he stood erect and gripped her arms tensely.

"You said you were in trouble. What kind of trouble? Who killed that Martian soldier in the corridor?"

"I did. I had to. He was guarding the cruiser—they've put a guard on everything now, since your escape."

"But why?" asked Brand. "What was so urgent on this ship that made you kill a man to get into it? Were you running away?"

"No. I wanted to send a radio message, and this is the only way I could do it without Jeff finding out where it came from, or who sent it."

"A message to whom?"

"To Commander Wilson. I knew he was your superior officer, and I had to know if you had escaped, and what you were doing. There's so much that has been going on while you were gone. Martin, they're almost ready. The attack will come any day now."

"Estelle," said Brand soberly. "I'm afraid there isn't much I can do about it. I'm in trouble too, and there's no way out. You see, Commander Wilson is dead. Officially, so is Martin Brand. In my identity as Robert Wales, I am a political criminal, and all record of my work as a Special Service agent is destroyed. I'm nobody, Estelle, except a nameless prospector wanted for murder by the Lunar police. I've got a job to do, and no one to help me do it. I've got to work entirely alone."

"What are you going to do?" she gasped.

"Just what you intended to do," said Brand. "I'm going to use that radio. But first, you must tell me something. Has there been any action down here? Has an Earth Patrol ship investigated? And if so, what happened to it?"

She shook her head.

"No. I'm sure of it. There has been no disturbance. But I do know that several more battleships have arrived, and many transports. They are strung in a long line straight down from this anchorage. They have sufficient force to invade Earth and subjugate it. The moon will be a simple matter. One battleship and one transport can take over the Lunar cities at will. The battleship will anchor at the center of the moon, command all the cities at long range, and blast those that refuse to surrender.

"The Martians will take over all the space ports, and fifth-columnists will aid in this work. Jeff said there were two hundred thousand fifth columnists waiting for the battleship to emerge and destroy the main entry shaft. That will be the signal for the fifth-column attack."

"But that's suicidal!" said Brand.

"How will they get the battleships out of the moon to attack Earth, with the main entry shaft gone? That's the only crater shaft large enough to admit such ships."

"They came in at Copernicus," said Estelle.

"*Copernicus?* Impossible! That crater has a solid bottom."

"No it hasn't. Martian engineers have been working on it for two years, constructing a huge shaft at an angle, so it isn't visible from above. Naturally no one ever visits that hellish hole."

"That's bad," said Brand. "Not even the Earth patrol will detect the Martians until they actually attack. Patrol ships don't cover the area between Earth and Luna."

"They'll win, Martin," said Estelle. "They'll *win.*"

There was a strange note in her voice and her trembling, strangely, had stopped.

"Maybe not," said Brand grimly. "Give me that flashlight. I'm going to try to pick up that patrol ship. I'm sure it's still searching somewhere in the Black Hole. I'll have to get him, or nobody. The radio in this cruiser won't penetrate the Lunar crust, and can't reach the Earth."

Estelle gave him the flashlight, and he turned it on. He turned to the radio, and seated himself. He snapped on the switches, waited while the tubes warmed up, then pressed the sending switch.

"How do you know the wavelength?" asked Estelle curiously. Brand ignored her question for the moment. Instead he began calling tensely into the microphone.

"Robert Wales calling Patrol Ship N-twenty-seven. Calling Patrol Ship N-twenty-seven. Robert Wales calling Patrol Ship N-twenty-seven. Please come in, N-twenty-seven. Urgent. Please come in…"

"N-twenty-seven, answering Robert Wales," a voice suddenly crackled from the receiver. "Who the hell are you, and where are you?"

"Never mind who I am," said Brand. "Where are you?"

"Nice work, if you can get it," said the voice from the ether. "Hold on a minute, I'll call Captain Craig. He'll talk to you."

"There *is* an Earth Patrol ship in the Black Hole," gasped Estelle.

"Sure…" Brand turned to her with a curious look. "What's so odd about that? It was sent in here to investigate and it never came out, so it's still here."

"But who sent it?" asked Estelle.

"Certainly you wouldn't—it would be suicide, if they did find the battleships. Why, in one second they could be blasted to bits."

"I know, and I didn't send it. Kathleen…"

"Captain Craig calling Robert Wales," came a familiar voice from the radio. "What is your message?"

"Listen, Captain," said Brand urgently. "Radio Earth and tell them to send a task force to blockade Copernicus crater, and to investigate escape shaft at its bottom. Martian battleships are planning to emerge from it to attack Earth. This attack may be soon…"

*"I recognize your voice,"* said Captain Craig in sharp interruption. "So you're using your real name now, eh? Before it was Martin Brand. I checked on that again, you lousy traitor. Martin Brand is dead and buried, as official as hell. And you are an exile from Earth because of seditious acts. Come again, Wales. If you think an Earth task force will be lured into any Copernicus trap, you're mistaken. I'll call Earth all right, and the whole Patrol will be out after your hide."

"Captain," said Brand angrily, "you are a fool. Do you think it's logical that anybody could hope to gain from the destruction of any single Earth unit? I tell you, the danger is urgent. So long as you are in the Black Hole right now, you have the opportunity to check. If I show you a fleet of Martian battleships, will you believe me?"

"I've got eyes," said Captain Craig, "and from the sound of you, you're pretty close to us. What did you do to Miss

Dennis?" There was a hard, cold, furious note in the patrol captain's voice.

"I left her in Luna City, where she took me to the hospital…"

*"You skunk,"* Captain Craig's voice blasted from the receiver. "So you're Edgar Barnes too. I picked that up on the radio just a few hours ago. Killed an Earth citizen, kidnapped a taxi-driver, marooned him in a crater, and left him to die. Only he didn't die. He got out, and came to the police with enough to hang you…"

"Listen, you stupid ape," said Brand slowly. "I'll give myself up to you right now, if you want to come and get me, but when you pick me up, you'll also see those battleships. This is the only way I can carry out my work. Commander Wilson had me covered, but an explosion and fire destroyed any evidence I had to prove my identity. You can believe what you wish—Martin Brand, Edgar Barnes, or Robert Wales. Now if you'll point your ship wherever you are, in the direction of Luna city, and keep your eyes open, you'll see something very soon. As soon as you see it, I'll be coming at you from that source, to come aboard. After that, the rest is up to you."

There was a moment's hesitation from the receiver, then the voice of the captain came again.

"Whoever you are," he said slowly, "you sure sound sincere. Okay, buddy. Show me something, and I'll radio Earth so fast it'll singe the hair off every Martian on Luna."

"Attaboy, Captain," said Martin Brand thankfully. "And one more thing, whatever you do, don't come too close. You can't beat what's lying here, and I would like to get out alive, if possible. I've got a friend here, who…" Brand turned to smile triumphantly up at Estelle and broke off in mid-sentence. "She's gone!" he gasped.

"Who's gone?" asked Captain Craig's voice.

"Never mind," yelled Brand.

"Watch in the direction of Luna City for fireworks, right down in the Black Hole. I've got to stop that girl…she's gone after Jeffry Killian…"

He snapped off the key and whirled toward the doorway. He plunged down the corridor recklessly, stumbled over the corpse of the Martian guard, and reached the gangplank.

As he stepped down to the dock, a brilliant searchlight beam winked on, and caught him full in its brilliance.

"Put up your hands," came a shout. "Don't move another step." Brand halted, baffled and angry.

Several Martian soldiers came out of the darkness and gripped his arms. They marched him along toward the caverns he had once escaped from. Their faces were grim.

"You didn't know when you were well off," said one.

"Yes," said the other. "When Miss Carter gets hold of you, you'll be worse off than before. She's really doing a job running this show. An order from her is as good as one from the Commander, himself. I gotta hunch it'll be Mr. and Mrs. Jeffry Killian, governors of America, or something like that, when we smash the Earth in a couple of days. Smart, that dame…"

Brand's blood ran cold in his veins.

"What's that you say?" he faltered.

The Martian laughed hoarsely.

"Say, did you think you had a chance with that baby? She's ice. I don't know how she does it: Maybe it's because she was crazy once. She sure isn't now. Why the other day…"

*"Look out!"* screamed the other guard. "Lu-bats!"

The sweeping rush of wind that betokened the dive of one of the monsters of the Black Hole screamed down at them on the narrow ledge. One of the guards lifted his atomic rifle and began firing blindly.

"There's more than one!" screamed the guard again. "There're three, at least. We'll never get 'em in time… We're done…"

"Steam-guns!" shouted Brand. "Train your steam guns on the carcass, you fools. They can be blown up that way."

"That's right," shouted one of his former captors, now shrinking back against the cavern wall, trying to pull his steam gun out of its holster. "You pulled that trick before, didn't you…?"

Brand snatched the pistol from his grasp, trained it aloft, and pressed the trigger. The other guard was doing the same. The scream of the wind from the diving lu-bats was a shriek in their ears now, as they came down to the attack. They had undoubtedly been attracted by the searchlight, whose beams still bathed the docks and the pathway.

Suddenly the lu-bat Brand had concentrated on blew up with a terrific roar and a blinding flash of flame that communicated itself to one of its two companions, and it too went off with a thunderous blast.

But the other lu-bat came on, seemingly oblivious of the holocaust of brilliance around it that now lit up the crater for ten miles around. Desperately Brand added the fire of his steam gun to that of the other guard, and suddenly the combined beams took effect. A third flaming carcass came plunging down like a meteor, to flash past into the depths, only a few yards from them.

A hoarse scream of agony came from the guard with the steam gun, and a large flaming fragment crashed down squarely on him. He screamed horribly once, then plunged off the ledge into the depths, a seared corpse.

Brand whirled, half-blinded by the light, and raced down the pathway toward the docks. An atomic rifle bullet exploded just behind him, sending a cloud of rock splinters into his back that struck with numbing force. Brand whirled, flicked up his steam gun, caught the Martian soldier squarely in the chest. He went down, dead before he hit the rocky trail.

At the other end of the dock, a small cruiser darted out toward one of the battleships and Brand cursed.

"Who the hell..."

Then it dawned on him and he went white.

"Estelle..." he choked. "She's in that ship..."

He stumbled on down to the cruiser, and clambered into it. He shut the door, and made his way to the control room. Just as he reached it, he saw Estelle's ship reach the side of the monster war-craft, saw it slip into an air lock that opened to receive her.

Brand snapped open the radio key, waited impatiently while the tubes warmed up, but as he waited, he slammed home the motor levers and drew the ship away from the dock. He cursed when the ship stopped with a jolt. He'd forgotten to cast off the mooring cable.

His finger pressed down savagely, and as the cruiser leaped away, half the dock tumbled into the abyss of the crater behind him, and he grinned. Perhaps that hadn't been a half-bad mistake, at that. Now any pursuers couldn't reach the other cruisers to take off after him.

He sent the cruiser hurtling at right angles away from the huge battleship. Now that the lu-bat carcasses had disappeared into the depths, their brilliant flames extinguished, he lost himself in the blackness that had resulted.

Pressing the radio key, he called anxiously into it.

"Martin Brand calling Captain Craig, Patrol Ship, N-Twent…"

"I hear you!" came the excited voice from the receiver. "And boy, I see you too! We're only a dozen miles away, straight out. Get off the air, Brand, or Wales, or whoever you are, I'm radioing Earth headquarters."

"Go ahead," yelled Brand. "And start running. If those battleships spot you, it'll be curtains. Full speed away. Quick!"

He snapped off the radio and sent the cruiser flashing along the crater wall. When he reached a spot where a sort of indentation offered concealment, he edged into it. Then he stopped the ship and waited. He listened intently to the radio, heard Craig's voice calling urgently into his transmitter.

"Patrol Ship N-twenty-seven, calling headquarters," he barked. "N-twenty-seven calling Earth Come in, Earth headquarters."

Suddenly a brilliant beam of light cut through the Black Hole as a searchlight on one of the battleships—the one Estelle had boarded—flashed on. A moment it flicked through the void like a giant sword, then suddenly it caught a tiny mote, lost it once, then held it fast.

"Damn," said Brand, clenching his fists. "They've spotted the N-twenty-seven."

A flash came from the battleship, and Brand could follow the course of it along the searchlight beam, saw it end at the tiny fleeing mote. There was a brilliant burst of flame, and the voice of Captain Craig in the receiver cut off abruptly.

And as its echoes died, Brand realized the truth—the message had not gotten through. Earth had not yet replied to its patrol ship's call.

Martin Brand sat in stunned silence for several long moments. Now, when he'd been just on the verge of the success of his mission, failure had blanked him out as completely as he had ever been. The luck of "Suicide" Martin Brand had come to an end.

The Earth was entirely unaware of the danger that threatened it. Estelle had tricked him. She had played up to him, fooled him with caresses. He thought almost subconsciously, with strange agony, of the red hair and the blue eyes of Kathleen Dennis, and a strange pang struck into his breast. A great anger was beginning to grow inside him, and it expressed itself in words now; words full of bitterness and hate that echoed through the silence of the control room.

"She wasn't sane. No sane person could have acted that superbly. Her mind might have regained its functions, but all the good in her, if there ever was any, had been killed. She was…"

He found no word to describe her.

Suddenly the radio receiver crackled and a voice came over it.

"Estelle Carter, calling Martin Brand," came the soft tones, but soft only in the sense that they were not loudly spoken.

In a sort of stupefied surprise, Brand clicked open the switch and answered. "What can I do for you now?" he said sarcastically.

"I, too, remembered the wavelength," her soft voice came to him mockingly. "And I am sitting in the control room, speaking over the private radio of the Commander of the Martian Invasion Fleet Enroute to Earth. In a few hours, I will take off to blast the Lunar entrance, and take control of the inner world. The rest of the fleet will proceed, under my orders, through Copernicus to Earth, to destroy the defenses. Earth will have to surrender in a matter of hours.

"Then, because it was I who did it, I will be able to dictate my own terms. I shall rule the Earth as the representative of the Martian government, I shall be truly an empress of the world, as there never has been before."

"You're mad!" said Brand.

"No," she said in the same level tones. "Mad once, but not now. Today I am the sanest person alive. I am, I realize it now, the ultimate example of sanity. All people have some insanity in their make-up. I have none. Everything but absolute logic has been erased from my brain. I am not hindered by emotion, although I understand fully what it is, and can simulate it if necessary. You should know that.

"If you had been as I am, you would not have been tricked by your emotions. You would have seen through my empty kisses, because, in the light of cold reason, they had no foundation. But you let your body rule your reason. You responded, and forgot to think…"

"You're possessed by the devil…" croaked Brand.

"I am a sane, logical, steady-minded human being. Perhaps, the only one who has ever lived."

"What…how did you do what you have done?" he asked.

"Remember the Martian you found dead in the ship in which you now sit?"

"Yes."

"I told him that he could rule Earth with me, so he killed Jeffry Killian for me, while I watched. It was very interesting to see him die, knowing that he was paying for what he did to me ten years ago. Perhaps that is the only emotion that I still retain to a slight degree, the ability to hate. But when it is satisfied by revenge, it is a very pleasurable emotion."

Brand listened with horror to this cold recital, but it was not finished. She went on:

"I had persuaded Jeffry Killian to commission me as his first lieutenant, and now, with him dead, I was able to take command without question. So under the ruse of going out to the flagship to take over command, I led my Martian friend to the cruiser, and told him the truth. Then I shot him in the face. He was a very surprised Martian.

"I told the truth when I said I was calling Commander Wilson. I wanted to know where you were. You have proved a pastime for me more than once, and I would have been very interested in making you become a traitor for love of me. But this way is better. I don't intend to bother you again. You are in a situation that is perfect. Even I could not have figured out a better predicament. It will be interesting to watch what happens to you."

But Martin Brand was no longer listening to the mocking voice. Lurking in the depths of his mind was a response to this jumble of words he'd heard.

He sent the cruiser out into the Black Hole, all lights doused, and drove it back toward the giant battleship.

The voice of Estelle Carter went on.

"Are you listening, Martin Brand?"

"Yes," he said grimly.

"Good. I am curious to know who Kathleen is. Could it be that the heart-broken, bitter, savage soldier of space found a new love after all? If you did, then it must have been a weak love indeed, to wilt that moment I threw myself into your arms."

Brand did not answer. Instead he was intent on a giant black bulk looming up ahead of him. He dipped the cruiser down, proceeding slowly and silently in the darkness.

"I see you do not answer me," mocked Estelle. "You are afraid that I will find her and do something to her. That is silly. If she really loves you, and you her, I would not think of destroying the beauty of that love, and the trials and tribulations it will have to endure because of the intolerable situation that exists for you.

"Certainly you can never make her happy. You can never marry her. You can only face the reality of being nobody at all. You haven't even a name you can call your own. As Martin Brand you are dead. As Robert Wales you are a traitor and seditionist, with no rights of citizenship on any world, therefore no right to marry. As Edgar Barnes, you are a murderer, and as such, will be executed if caught, according to Lunar law."

The mocking voice went on. Brand's jaw tightened as he listened, and he finally maneuvered the cruiser beneath the tremendous belly. Finally he had the ship hanging motionless, then he spoke.

"Listen, Estelle," he said quietly. "I've been letting you talk on, listening to you gloat over me. It's been very interesting to me. I can, of course, only judge you on an emotional basis, since I am not as 'sane' as you are. To me, your present condition is something to pity, and if I feel anything at all about you now, it is a large measure of sympathy.

"I am sure you are not responsible for your actions, and although for a moment I felt that I hated you, now I only pity you. I must destroy you because your warped mind is the most dangerous thing that has ever faced Earth's peace and happiness, and threatened it with permanent destruction.

"Mars may conquer Earth, but wars come and go, and freedom is won again. But if you were to come in power, with your mad mentality, then indeed a sad thing would happen to the world I love.

"That is why I am going to destroy you now!"

For a moment there was silence, then Estelle's voice came to him coldly, with short-clipped words coming from her lips like venom from the fangs of a snake.

"It is you who are mad now, Martin Brand! You speak wildly of destroying. You can destroy nothing. You sit there in a tiny ten-man cruiser, hiding like a rat in some hole in the wall. You have at your disposal one small cannon, which fires an atomic shell capable of smashing only a small destroyer. What can you do to me here in the mightiest battleship in all the solar system? You..."

Martin Brand interrupted.

"That atomic cannon you speak of is pointing at the moment straight into the bomb rack of your mighty ship. It will send that atomic shell you speak of straight into the magazine of your battleship. And when it explodes..."

"You lie!" shrieked Estelle Carter. "You lie! You are nowhere near."

"Before you die," said Brand, "there is one thing you can think of. What is that emotion in your voice now? I'd call it fear. Fear is a terrible thing, Estelle, and because I pity you, I don't intend to let you suffer any longer. My finger is on the trigger..."

Martin Brand pressed the trigger, and with the other hand sent the tiny ten-man cruiser peeling off in a tremendous swooping dive straight out and down into the Black Hole's depths. Behind him a great mushrooming flame grew and grew until it seemed that it would catch up to him and destroy him too. But it tossed him on, like a feather before a gale, and his senses reeled with the awful sensation of a dive almost more than human tissue can stand.

Even through the reeling of his mind, he heard the thunder of the holocaust he had set off behind him. All was flame and light and smoke and bursting sound in the Black Hole. And added to it was a new thunder that was not that of rending metal, but of shattering rock.

He brought the buffeted cruiser to a steadier pace, and looked back when his sight had cleared enough to see what had happened behind him.

Like a slow-motion move, the whole wall of the crater was toppling over, engulfing all the cataclysmic holocaust of shattered ships as though it had been but a match-flame in the darkness. And many minutes later the whole mass came to rest on the side of the crater and once more darkness fell over the scene.

The Martian armada was no more.

And then, Martin Brand, desperate daredevil of space, bowed his head in his hands and cried.

The lights of Luna City were bright before him, several hours later, as he brought the cruiser slowly forward. In his mind were crowding the memories of the past hours, and he gave no thought to his own situation. Nor did he do more than glance idly at the small ship that bore down on him now from above and behind. It was only when his radio crackled, and a voice came through the receiver, that he stirred, and the grim immobility of his features changed.

"Lunar patrol ship A-forty calling cruiser below us—land at Luna City spaceport and no tricks. We'll blast you if you make a move."

Brand drove the ship slowly toward the spaceport and brought it down. The patrol ship landed behind him, and he stepped out to meet the two figures who climbed from it. One of them was familiar, clad in the trim uniform of an Earth Patrol agent, red hair gleaming under smart military cap, and blue eyes expressionless in her white face…Kathleen Dennis.

The officer spoke.

"Robert Wales, alias Edgar Barnes, I arrest you for murder, for attempted sabotage, and for conspiring to destroy the peace of Luna and Earth."

Martin Brand scarcely heard the charges. He was staring at Kathleen Dennis, at the hurt in her eyes, at the disgust on her face, and at the stiff unyielding posture of her trimly uniformed figure.

"Why are you looking at me like that?" he said.

*"You are a traitor!"* she said in a low voice.

Brand reeled in shock, then stepped forward.

"What do you mean?" he asked.

"Captain Craig radioed the whole story to Luna Headquarters just before his radio blanked out, just before you shot him down with that Martian cruiser you smuggled into the Black Hole."

"He was shot down by the Martians," Brand burst out. "I blew up the magazine of the flagship, and the whole fleet was buried beneath a slide in the Black Hole..."

"That'll be enough," interrupted the Lunar officer. "Come along, Robert Wales. You are under arrest, and I promise you, this time you won't just be exiled. It's execution for you."

"But I tell you it's true. That's what Captain Craig was trying to radio to Earth headquarters—that he had seen those battleships in the Black Hole. They were ready to attack. Estelle Carter, completely mad, was in command..."

Kathleen's eyes opened wide.

"I see it all now," she said. "I heard that she was released as cured..." She turned to the Lunar officer. "This man was exiled from Earth for sedition. He has attempted the same thing here. He has claimed to be Martin Brand, whom you know is dead. It was Martin Brand's old sweetheart he just mentioned. Somewhere he got hold of that, and tried to use it to his own advantage. He is a traitor, and I leave him in your hands."

"We'll take care of him," promised the Lunarian grimly. "He won't be exiled again."

Kathleen turned to Martin Brand.

In her eyes he saw a light that he himself had in his own eyes ten years ago.

"I have a job to do," she said, "and I intend to *do* it." Then she turned and stalked swiftly away. Martin Brand found his wrists encircled by a pair of handcuffs.

He stared down at them and a whisper escaped his lips.

"The luck of 'Suicide' Martin Brand!" he murmured. "It's run out at last."

He looked at her disappearing back.

"It's all right, Kathleen. You'll get over it. But maybe someday you'll know that I had a job to do too, and I *did* it just as you think you are doing yours now in condemning a dangerous traitor."

## CHAPTER ELEVEN

It was silent in the tomb. Hal Orson, still deep in thought, became aware that Kathleen's sobs had died away as she stirred restlessly in his arms.

"I'm all right now, Hal."

He released her almost automatically. She looked up at his intent face in the glow of the black light lamp.

"What is it, Hal…?"

"So—they lied to us," he said, a baffled note in his voice. "But why?" He sat down on the marble slab where it lay beside the empty coffin of a Martin Brand who was believed dead by three worlds. Why was it empty? Was it because …

"He isn't dead," said Kathleen in a whisper. "That's why they lied. There would be no other reason for it. If he had been executed on Luna as a murderer and a spy, there would have been no reason to lie about Martin Brand's body..."

Orson nodded. "I get all that. We of the Service knew Martin wasn't in that tomb to begin with, that his death had been faked. This would avoid any possibility of Luna's linking Robert Wales with Martin Brand, and therefore with Earth politics, and thus uncover the secret of the Special Services and its work on Luna. But why didn't they leave it that way? All of us would have understood anything but this..."

"It's simple," said Kathleen. "This way, with everybody in the Service believing that Martin's body had actually been recovered from Luna—and put into the tomb it was supposed to occupy, no legend would be built up about it. No possibility of the fact that it really was empty could get out. It was just a logical precaution."

Orson rose to his feet. "Then *where* is he? He was useless to the Service for any further work. There'd be no reason to keep away from me. I was his best friend..."

"I know why," said Kathleen calmly. "It's because he *wasn't* useless. It's because he's still working for the Service. I know it, as sure as I'm a woman."

"How?"

"Intuition...and because you can't love a man for eleven years as I have, without getting so close mentally that you can sense whether he's alive or dead. I *know* he's alive. I can...*feel* him."

Orson laid a hand on her arm, gently. "Kathleen, you're a clever girl. You must be able to see the other possibility— that what you feel might just be wishful thinking. Love does strange things to the mind, sometimes..."

She whirled and pointed to the coffin. "Is *that* wishful thinking?" she demanded. "What strange thing is happening to *your* mind that makes you see an empty coffin when it's *really* not empty…"

"Score for you," said Orson. "I'm not seeing things—that coffin's empty. And there's only one reason for that. What that reason is, we're going to find out…" He stopped suddenly and groaned. "Kathy, we've got to get out of here and work fast. Tomorrow, when all this havoc is discovered, there'll be hell to pay. If we're asked, where will we say we were tonight?"

"This wasn't your idea," she said calmly. "We were in my apartment."

"You say a thing like that, and I'll beat the tar out of you. You won't throw your reputation to the dogs to shield me. I'm no baby, either, Kathy, and don't forget it."

"I'm not going to let you get into trouble over me."

"I'm not going to *try* to keep out of trouble. Tomorrow I'm going to *make* trouble!"

"What are you thinking of?" she said sharply. "Whatever it is, I forbid it."

He grinned at her. "Go ahead and forbid. You don't scare me at all. There's nothing you can do."

She regarded him silently a moment. "Oh, isn't there?"

"No, there isn't. And now, we're getting out of here…"

He led the way out into the night.


"I'm sorry, Mr. Orson, but the first available time on Senator Beasley's appointment list is three weeks from today. You can't possibly see him before then."

"Will you pick up that phone," urged Orson, "and simply say Martin Brand can't wait three weeks?"

The secretary looked at Orson, then shrugged. "Maybe after a cryptic remark like that, he'll never want to see you, but if you insist…"

"I insist."

The secretary lifted the phone and spoke rapidly into it. Then his eye brows lifted and he put the receiver down. He'll take you in," he said. "Senator Beasley said he'd see you immediately. Whoever Martin Brand is—" The secretary stopped short. "Not the Martin Brand in the rifled tomb!" he exclaimed. "Mister, if you're using this as a gag to see the senator, I'd advise you to start running now, because you'll be in real trouble."

Orson grinned. "Wouldn't you like to know."

The secretary flushed and led Orson to a door. He opened it and let Orson through it. Then he backed out, shut the door behind him. Orson faced the man at the desk, a large man with bristling eyebrows and square jaw.

"Sit down," said the senator.

Orson sat down in the chair opposite the desk and remained quiet while the senator eyed him.

"You know," said Senator Beasley, "there's no name more unusual for announcing yourself than that of a famous deceased hero. I should say that unless you have a very good reason I may be forced to ask you quite a few questions."

"When I've asked you the ones I want to ask," said Orson, "I'll be glad to answer any you wish to ask. First, I've read the papers, and I know what they say."

"What do they say?" asked Beasley, folding his hands across his expansive stomach.

"They say that the body of Martin Brand has been stolen from its mausoleum," said Orson. "Only it wasn't."

Senator Beasley slumped down a trifle more in his chair, and his voice remained deep and calm. "You were with her, then?" he asked.

Orson stiffened with surprise in his chair. "With *her...?*"

"Yes. And you know, as she does, that the coffin never had a body in it," Beasley concluded.

Orson looked at the senator ruefully. "Guess there's not much I can tell you, then," he said, "but how you know, beats me. Where'd you get your information?"

"Fingerprints. You and the girl left them all over the place. Hers were easy to classify, and the identification was placed on my desk an hour ago. I've been expecting your classification to arrive any minute. But you said something about wanting to ask me some questions before I questioned you. I'd be glad to answer them."

"You would?"

Senator Beasley smiled. "Of course. Did you think I'd refuse?"

Orson shrugged. "I don't know what to think. I haven't known what to think ever since I found the coffin empty. You see, Martin Brand was my best friend. I've always mourned him as dead, and it's been something of a shock to find that he wasn't. I don't understand it, sir, and least of all do I understand his not contacting me. That's the first question, sir: where is Martin Brand?"

"On Venus—where Kathleen will be in a few days, unless we stop her."

Orson leaped to his feet. "Kathleen—on Venus! But that's impossible, sir. I just left her a few hours ago."

Beasley unfolded his hands, picked up a piece of paper from his desk and handed it to Orson. "I presume you are the person for whom this was intended," he said. "We found it in her wastebasket."

Orson snatched the paper. It was unsigned but it was unmistakably in Kathleen's handwriting. It read: *There is only one place he could be, and I am going there. Stay out of it.*

Senator Beasley spoke. "I assume it was her idea, judging from that note."

"But it doesn't say Venus," said Orson. "How do you assume that's what she meant? And I'm in it as much as she is."

"Is she in love with him?"

"With a broken heart," emphasized Orson.

"And are you in love with her?"

Orson stared at the senator. "In love with her—? You mean you think that's why I helped her?"

"Is it?"

Orson looked thoughtful. "If Martin were dead, maybe I might think of it. But now that he's alive…"

"I see. Well, lad, let's have the rest of those questions."

"Why has the government resorted to this—this flummery?"

"The government hasn't resorted to it. I handled the whole thing—at the request of the President. You, I presume, are a member of Special Services?"

"I joined when Martin was—killed."

"Then you know why it was done, and why only the President and I know there was no body to be stolen," said Beasley. "Now we'll have to resort to some more flummery—and pretend to find the body, apprehend the grave robbers, and restore Mr. Brand to his mythical resting place."

"You're being quite frank," said Orson. "Why?"

"Because you are the grave robber," said Beasley quietly. "I'm afraid that with the evidence, including your own confession, nobody'd listen to a crazy story that the tomb was empty—especially when we find the body where you hid it."

Orson sat quietly for a moment, considering the senator. "I see," he said finally. "It's an excellent bit of—flummery. But I have one more question…"

"Ask it."

"Can I go to Venus too?"

There was a long silence in the room, and finally the senator seemed to have made a decision. He leaned forward and pressed a button on his desk.

"Just as soon as you've been executed," he said.

## CHAPTER TWELVE

Kathleen sat sipping a cocktail in the bar of the Venus de Milo cafe in Venus City. She remembered the weird experience of flying her own private ship into the milky atmosphere of Venus, almost sixty miles in depth, where visibility was still as much as twenty miles, and coming out finally from the stratosphere into the perpetual rosy dawn-light that is Venus' day. She still marveled at the pink orb of the sun, a vague rosy spot in the milk-white.

She remembered, too, the glimpse she had caught of the Patrol ship slipping quietly out of the milk-and-honey twenty miles behind her. She was almost sure they had been following her, and yet she had cleared the spaceport without the slightest trouble. She'd gambled on that—the Special Service wouldn't have risked publicity by trying to stop her officially—they'd stop her some other way. So she'd left the tarmac as soon as her papers had cleared. That had been several days ago.

Now, sitting in the Venus de Milo, she felt sure they'd never recognize her. Her coppery hair was jet black, her eyes were slanted back, pulled into that position by invisible strips of tape that were concealed by her hairdo. Her fingers were joined by tiny webs that extended halfway out to the first knuckles, and the tiny moons in her fingernails were a brilliant green in color. Her complexion was faintly green also, as though her blood had been tinted beneath the skin, as indeed it had. This effect was achieved by a new chlorophyll dye that turned the red corpuscles green without impairing their oxygen-carrying abilities. This effect would last for several days before a renewed injection of dye was necessary.

From all outward appearances, Kathleen was a Venusian, her disguise so perfect that not even a Venusian could detect any difference. She knew, however, that a member of Special Services would have little trouble spotting her. She was counting on the necessity for secrecy about the Special Service to protect her until she had discovered what she wanted to know.

Seated around a table in a corner of the cafe were four Venusians, conversing rapidly in low tones. Kathleen had been watching them ever since they came in, just as she had watched them the first day. Now they seemed to be aware of her. Several times she caught them glancing in her direction, and conversing with faint frowns immediately thereafter.

Finally one of them got up and sauntered toward her. Kathleen watched him come, observing his reflection in the big mirror behind the bar. There was something oddly familiar about him, but try as she would, she could not place him. He was a Venusian, that was apparent, for a Martian could not possibly pose as a Venusian—she started—or he could be an Earthman in disguise. As he seated himself beside her, she was suddenly sure of it. Inwardly she felt an exultation; it meant she was on the right track. She knew now that the four were fifth columnists.

"You're new here, aren't you?" the man asked, his voice strangely husky and familiar. There was a haunting timbre to it that wandered through her memory, as though searching for something.

"I don't believe I know you," she said, regarding his reflection in the glass, then sipping her drink casually.

He grinned at her. "That can be remedied," he said, "besides it's a shame for so lovely a girl to be drinking alone."

"I don't make friends easily—with strangers," she said, turning to look at him. As her eyes met his, that haunting sensation of familiarity heightened, and a tremor shot through her body. Suddenly she found herself breathing more swiftly, and for no real reason she felt afraid. Of what? Not of a Venusian spy, or a Martian fifth columnist—or of her life…What then?

He half-turned on his stool. "Then perhaps we'd better remain strangers," he said. "I don't judge people by their names—and actually names mean nothing, so, if you'd prefer…" He slid off the stool with a polite nod.

"Wait," she said.

He stood looking at her.

"Now that you're here, you might as well have a drink with me."

"Why?"

Kathleen stared at him in surprise. Suddenly she felt a surge of anger rise in her throat. He was looking at the slow flood of green suffusing her white throat, and strangely there was a look of scorn in his eyes.

"What kind of a man are you?" she flared.

"Generally I like to be alone," he said. "I'm a very bad judge of female character—and perhaps I've judged wrong again. If you'll pardon me…" He bowed slightly, stiffly, and made his way back to his three companions.

Kathleen tossed off her drink with an angry gesture, then climbed down from her stool and marched over to the table. She faced the Venusian squarely. "My name," she said stiffly, "is Kay deNees. And I like to be alone too." She turned and walked stiffly from the cafe. As she passed a large mirror near the doorway, she saw the Venusian staring at her retreating back. In his eyes was a peculiar expression and he looked puzzled, as though he were trying to remember something also. Kathleen frowned. She felt more sure than ever now that somewhere before she had seen this Venusian—and he hadn't been a Venusian then. Who was he? As she walked slowly down the street outside, she searched her memory diligently, but without success.

So occupied was she with her thoughts that she was unaware of the swift approach of a dark figure until strong arms lifted her off her feet and hustled her toward a waiting car. She screamed shrilly once then a belated hand clapped over her mouth. She promptly bit the hand and screamed again. As she was thrust into the waiting car and seized by two Earthmen, she saw the door to the cafe burst open. The man who had accosted her at the bar dashed out and stood watching as the car drove away in a burst of speed.

For a moment Kathleen was silent, studying the faces of her captors. "For Special Services men, you aren't very efficient," she observed. "You let me scream my head off. If Commander Wilson were alive, you'd be doing guard duty as buck privates back in Kansas City."

Suddenly she slumped down in the seat and began to cry. "Now I'll never find him," she said, her voice muffled by her sobs. "Why couldn't you let me alone?"

One of the men handed her a handkerchief. "You'd have been dead by tomorrow morning if we hadn't snatched you, Miss Dennis. You just don't know what you were getting into. That mob had you spotted, and our man reported this morning they were going to check you today. If you didn't measure up you'd be eliminated as a precautionary measure. And, who are you trying to find? ...Say! Don't tell me you're looking for the guy who stole Martin Brand's body? If you are, you're behind the times. They found the body the day after you left Earth, and the man who stole it has been executed. If you ask me, the dirty grave-robber got off easy..."

The Special Services man stopped speaking in alarm and stared at Kathleen's white face. "Joe," he said to his companion, "she really did love the guy. She's fainted."

His companion began to chafe Kathleen's wrists. "Yeah," he said, sympathetically. "Ain't it a shame some people never get any breaks? Imagine a girl taking chances with her life this way looking for the body of her dead lover. She must have known it was just plain suicide…"

Several hours later Kathleen sat staring at the plain furnishings of an office in the Federal Building. Her mind refused to consider the horrible news she had heard, and her eyes were dry. So, when the door opened and a man entered, she paid him scarce attention.

"How do you feel now?" the newcomer asked.

"All right, I suppose," said Kathleen dully. Then she turned to look at her visitor and stiffened in shock. The man facing her was one of the Venusians she had been spying upon at the Venus de Milo cafe.

"Yes," he said. "I thought you'd recognize me. Actually, however, I'm Don Coleridge, a member of Special Services. I've been on the inside with the fifth column for several months now. So, when you showed up, I knew the score."

"What are you doing here, then?" she asked, wonderingly. "Won't this spoil everything for you?"

"I don't think they'll find out. But…I had to do something—don't you realize you were under suspicion? When the decision was made to kill you, I had to act to save your life. So I notified my superior officer and had you arrested. That way, we hope, suspicion will be thrown off you."

Kathleen shrugged. "What good will it do now? I'm useless to everybody."

"Not at all. You'll find out about that in a few minutes. I'm going to leave now, but my purpose in coming here was to prove to you that I am on your side. Next time we meet, you'll know that, but you won't give any sign. From now on, you're working with me."

"Working with you?"

The disguised Venusian nodded and turned toward the door. "The superior officer will give you the details of the plan. Meanwhile, best of luck. And remember, I'll be handling the affair from the other end so you needn't be frightened. When you see me again, I will be Lieutenant Forsythe." He bowed himself out and closed the door.

An instant later the door opened again. A man stepped in backward and closed the door before he turned.

"Hal!" shrieked Kathleen. "Hal Orson!"

"Not so loud," said Orson in consternation. "Nobody here knows I'm Hal Orson."

Kathleen rushed forward and threw herself into his arms. "They told me you'd been executed," she gasped. "Oh Hal, I've been going through hell thinking about it."

"I know," he said, disengaging himself gently, "but it had to be that way."

Kathleen stood looking at him for an instant, then her eyes clouded and she sat down and cried quietly for a few moments. Orson stood looking down at her silently until she had finished.

"Ready for work now?"

She looked up at him and nodded. "What kind of work?"

Orson sat down beside her. "That Venusian who was just in to see you," he explained, "is one of our men. He's gotten pretty high in the enemy intelligence circle and this is all his plan. He saved your life by pulling this fake arrest; now he's arranging to 'rescue' you."

"Rescue me?"

"Yes. Tonight you'll be placed in a cell in the Federal Building jail and about midnight a group of Venusian will raid the place to free you. They'll encounter little resistance, a careless guard, and a great deal of overconfidence on our part. They'll succeed in rescuing you. After that, you'll be, we hope, another member of the SS in the enemy circle.

"But what good will I be?" asked Kathleen.

Orson grinned at her. "What you've got is exactly what we need now. You have no idea how effective a beautiful woman will be in prying secrets from these Venusians. They go for a pretty face and figure like nobody's business. I think you know how to handle yourself to best advantage there."

Kathleen frowned. "I'm not so sure. I've had a little experience with one of those fellows already. He gave me the most beautiful brush-off I've ever gotten. If you ask me, there are some Venusians who could make a marble Venus shiver in a steam bath."

"He was only the fellow picked to 'feel you out' as it were, and decide if you were spying on them or not. He had no intentions of making up to you."

Kathleen looked dubious. "He wasn't acting a part. That fellow really is a lone wolf. I played coy for just one sentence and he froze me off like…" Kathleen knit her eyebrows. "I've seen that man somewhere before, but I can't place him at all."

"Hmm," said Orson. "I don't like that…"

Kathleen looked at him quickly. "Never mind," she said. "It makes no difference. I'm sure he doesn't know me. The way he acted proved it. There'll be no danger."

Orson laughed dryly. "No *danger?* Kathy, you're in the most *dangerous* game in the Solar System now, and there's no doubt about it. We're all playing with the biggest potential explosion ever imagined—and if we don't manage to touch it off where it's harmless, it'll be the end for more than we few

SS men. Kathy, if we don't stop these fellows, it's curtains for Earth. What we've learned about what the Martians have on tap for us is…well, frightening. We've got to know when and where the first blow will fall, because the first blow will likely be the last. That's what you and I and Coleridge will be trying to find out."

"I'll do my best," said Kathleen.

Orson flashed a convincing smile and rose to go. "I know you will, Kathy. And Kathy…"

"Yes?"

"I don't know where, but I know for sure that Martin is on Venus right now, alive and well. Headquarters lost all track of him because he requested to be entirely on his own, and we won't hear from him until he has something positive to report, if by any chance you run across him."

Kathleen went white.

"…don't do anything to give either of you away," finished Orson. "Don't let on by the slightest sign that you know who he is, or let him know about you—until it's all over. Of course, I don't think you'll meet him—the chances are extremely remote—but if you do…"

"You don't think I'd risk his life again, do you, Hal?" Kathleen said in strained tones. "I'd die first…"

"I hope you don't," said Orson, wheeling abruptly and striding from the room.

## CHAPTER THIRTEEN

The long hours until midnight dragged interminably for Kathleen, lying on her bunk in the cell, trying desperately to get some sleep but failing utterly to compose her mind.

"Martin," she whispered into the darkness. "Oh Martin, if only I can find you—see you just once more…"

She lay there, thinking, her eyes full of tears, but her heart full of hope. Outside, in the corridor, the sound of footsteps aroused her. They stopped at her door, and she heard the sound of a key grating in the lock.

"Come on out, Miss deNees," said a soft voice. "We're taking you out of here."

She recognized the voice as that of Don Coleridge. As she stepped through the cell doorway, she saw the jailer standing with his arms slightly elevated, keeping a calculating and careful eye on the two men who stood beside him. One of two masked Venusians had a steam gun trained on the jailer. Kathleen decided this one was Don Coleridge.

"Thank you," she said. "I don't know why you're doing this, but I appreciate it."

"We can make mistakes too, sometimes," he said. "But come on, we've got to step lively. This is the quiet period around here, but it'll be tough if this fellow manages to spread the alarm. We'll just have to silence him for awhile…"

Swiftly he chopped down with his gun at the neck of the jailer, and with a moan the fellow dropped to the floor. The rescuers shoved him into the cell and locked the door, then motioned Kathleen to follow them down the corridor. They went down a side corridor and emerged finally in a driveway where a cab stood waiting. They got into it and the driver drew the car away from the curb without a word.

For several minutes no one spoke, then Don Coleridge removed his mask and placed it in his pocket.

His companion did the same. "That was almost too easy," he said.

Coleridge grunted. "It was, Farrow, but I guess we were lucky. Or, I should say, you were lucky, Miss deNees. Do you realize that you'd have been in the toughest spot imaginable if the Earthmen could have pinned anything concrete on you?"

Kathleen said nothing.

"Okay," acknowledged Coleridge. "At least you're smart. But, you can trust us, if you will. As a matter of fact, you have no other choice now. If you aren't on our side, you'll be in a much worse fix than if we'd left you there—but we figured anybody *they* were mad at, ought to be a friend of ours."

Kathleen shrugged. "I'm on nobody's side but my own. It's just that I hate Earthmen's guts—that's all."

Coleridge regarded her calculatingly for a moment. "Maybe you'd like a job," he said. "Maybe you'd like to do something they wouldn't enjoy."

"What's in it?" asked Kathleen.

Farrow laughed. "Money," he said. "Isn't that what you want?"

Kathleen read the inflection in his voice right, and turned to stare into his eyes. "Money isn't everything," she said. "But it's almost everything when you haven't got it. Can you think of a good substitute?"

The sudden glint that came into Farrow's eyes told Kathleen she was on the right track. He said nothing, however, and she sank back into her seat, satisfied that she had discovered at least one weak spot in the enemy armor.

The cab left the city. Once on the highway outside the residential area, it crept off onto a side road. There, in the dark, a transfer was made to an aero-car, which took off immediately on a course directly over the Venusian jungles.

Kathleen glanced at Coleridge and he interpreted her look correctly.

"Venus City is no place for any of us, from now on. We can't afford to take any chances. You'd be picked up in a minute back there. And we can't be sure how smart that jailer was, or how much he'll remember of us."

"Should have killed him," said Farrow.

"You're too bloodthirsty," said Coleridge.

"Not bloodthirsty; just practical and smart."

Coleridge looked at Farrow quizzically, but said nothing more. Kathleen felt a sudden misgiving and she tried to study Farrow without seeming to be too interested in him.

Several hours later the car set down in a tiny clearing in the forest, and the three made their way into a tiny hut. Inside, Coleridge touched a rustic table that was securely fastened to the floor. The entire floor began to sink slowly into the ground; they were on a cleverly concealed elevator.

At the bottom they stepped off. The floor returned to its original level, and as it did so, a light came on. Kathleen saw they were at the end of a dim tunnel that led a short way into the earth before it turned. They followed the tunnel and entered a large, brilliantly lighted room. It was plainly furnished. Behind a large desk sat a saturnine-faced Martian.

"Here they are, Sir," said Farrow, saluting.

Coleridge froze in his tracks for a brief instant, then saluted also and stood facing the Martian. Kathleen, gave Coleridge one swift glance, then faced the Martian. Something had gone wrong here—definitely wrong!

"You may go, Farrow," said the Martian.

Farrow saluted again. He whirled on his heel and walked back the way they had come. As he passed Coleridge and Kathleen he grinned knowingly, and one derisive whispered word reached their ears.

"Smart."

Coleridge tried to bluff it out. "This is Miss Kay deNees," he said. "She was picked up by Earth Secret Service men, so we decided we couldn't risk them keeping her. As it turned out, sir, she is perfectly willing to work with us, and in my opinion we can put her to good use."

The Martian smiled. "I'm sure we can. As a matter of fact, we have *already* put her to excellent use. You Earthmen can't keep your heads in the presence of a pretty woman. If you could, perhaps we'd never be able to detect a spy in our midst."

Coleridge had gone white, but Kathleen's eyes widened in astonishment and she whirled on Coleridge. "An Earthman!" she exclaimed. "Is this true?" Her astonishment turned to fury. "So, you tricked me. You Earthmen are all the same. Rescue me, will you! Now you've really gotten me into trouble. Whatever's going on here, it strikes me as pretty dangerous, but if it's what I think it is, I'm all for it—if that filthy, rotten mind of yours hasn't got me a jungle grave."

The Martian regarded her with amusement. "I can see, Miss deNees, why your superiors thought you could achieve success in a mission against us," he said. "You are clever, and a very good actress. Unfortunately for you, however, we have some clever men on our side. Mr. Farrow very neatly uncovered the whole plot. As a matter of fact, he even has a series of interesting microphotos of your consultation with your companion in espionage in the Federal building back in Venus City. When he showed them to me, I accepted his suggestion that we appear to fall for the plan, and bring about your rescue. That way, we'd bag both of you with a minimum amount of trouble—with actual SS assistance as a matter of fact."

The Martian pressed a buzzer and an orderly entered. "Send me Captain Lutain and ask Lieutenant Farrow to come back in, please."

In a moment Farrow and Lutain entered. Kathleen recognized the captain at once as the man who had accosted her at the Venus de Milo.

"Gentlemen," said the Martian, "we have here two spies. I am detailing one of them to each of you. Farrow, you will take the gentleman, and when you have taken him deep into the jungle, kill him and bury him in the quicksand. Lutain, you will do the lovely, if detestable, Miss deNees the same service."

Captain Lutain spoke up. "If you would be so kind," he said, "I'd rather you'd spare me the task sir. Were she an Earthwoman, I'd have no compunctions, but since she is a Venusian, I'd rather not."

The Martian laughed. "She's not a Venusian, but no matter. As a matter of fact, on second thought, I want to confer with you. Mission E is due to get underway on secret orders, which may come within forty-eight hours. I'll appoint another man."

Farrow saluted and spoke. "Sir, there will be no need. I can take care of both spies. I started this matter, and I'd like the honor of finishing it."

The Martian's eyes lit in approval. "You're a good man, Farrow, but you must use dispatch. As a member of Mission E, it will be necessary that you return before the orders come."

Farrow's eyes lighted with a feral glow. "I'll be here sir. I wouldn't miss being in on the big…"

"That will do, Farrow. You had best be quick about your assignment if you want to be sure of that."

Farrow smiled gloatingly and produced his steam pistol. "All right, you two," he said, "walk ahead of me down the corridor. I know a quicksand deposit only a few hours away…"

Kathleen, her heart in her throat, turned to walk down the corridor ahead of the prodding steam gun. She saw Captain Lutain staring at her again with that same puzzled look in his eyes. He took one impulsive step forward, then halted, shaking his head.

The Martian misinterpreted his motion, "Farrow can take care of it, Captain," he said with a wave of his hand. "Besides, I want to check a few things with you right now."

Kathleen squared her shoulders and marched into the gloomy corridor, a vague remembrance hammering at her memory for recognition, but there was no response—once more she failed to place the strange feeling she had when she looked at the Venusian captain.

The orderly standing before Commander Hal Orson's desk in the Federal Building at Venus City saluted.

"What is it?" asked Orson.

"There's a gentleman, a Venusian, here to see you, sir. He insists that it is extremely important, and he refuses to give his name."

Orson nodded. "All right. Send him in, but stay on guard with your steam gun ready. We've had enough trouble with Venusians here already."

The orderly wheeled and went out, returning in a moment with a Venusian dressed in plain clothes.

The Venusian halted in his tracks, a look of stunned astonishment on his face as he saw Orson. "My God," he said. "Hal!"

"That will be all," said Orson sharply. "Orderly, please withdraw, but remain on call." The orderly, withdrew.

Orson faced the Venusian. "Now," he said. "Who the devil are you?"

The Venusian grinned. "What's the matter, Hal? You seem mighty coy about your name, all of a sudden. Back on Earth, in the SS, you used it without any qualms—don't tell me you've got in trouble, too, and had to give up being yourself? And since when can't a man address his former bunkmate by his first name?"

"Martin?" exclaimed Orson. *"Martin Brand!"*

With one bound he was out from behind the desk and flung his arms around the tall figure. Then he grasped Martin's hand and pumped it up and down. "You old rascal," he almost sobbed. "You son of a gun. Damn your conscienceless hide…" He broke off, unable to continue.

"What are you doing here?" asked Brand, returning his handclasp with equal vehemence. "I hardly expected my old pal to be in command in Venus City."

"I'm not your old pal," said Orson. "I was executed for grave-robbing, back on Earth, and now I'm just as much a nonentity as you are. I'm a commander here because I know too much to be anywhere else. I know almost as much as you do about this affair."

"Grave-robbing?" asked Brand with a puzzled look. "What on Earth would you be doing robbing graves?"

Orson swallowed uncomfortably. "That's a long story, Martin, and…"

"Then it'll keep," said Brand. "What I've got to tell you is much more important, and I haven't much time. Hal, this is serious, the most serious thing that can happen; and we've only one way out. The Martians are sending in a big battleship, but it's the fastest thing in space, and there's not one chance in a million of intercepting it, or even of destroying it if we could intercept it—without knowing exactly what its course to Earth would be."

Orson looked puzzled. "One battleship? You mean they're attacking Earth with *one* ship? I can't see how that could make a great deal of difference even if they get through. It just can't get them anywhere…"

"*This* can. Hal, that ship is nothing but a generator ship— and the biggest thing you ever saw. It's sole purpose is to generate an impulse, from one Earth diameter out that will cover the whole globe. That impulse will detonate hydrogen-bombs concealed in every great city, in every important area on Earth. These bombs have been hidden during the past five years by Venusian freighters, traders, and importers. Once that generator ship gets within eight thousand miles of Earth, our power to resist will be ended. The Martians will be able to come in at will and take over."

Orson, his face gray, went back behind his desk and sat down heavily. "What will we do?" he asked. "What *can* we do?"

"I've been assigned to that detonator ship," said Brand. "I'm one of the most trusted men in the whole plan. Don't ask me how I did it. Take it from me, if it's humanly possible, that ship will not reach the Earth, or anywhere near it. I've made all my plans, and it's a one-man job. Even if I succeed, that would only remedy the matter temporarily. Another ship is nearly ready to go, and I've just learned where it is. You've got to finish things up here. You've got to destroy that ship and round up the fifth column on Venus. I've got a list and location of all the big shots here—" Brand tossed a notebook down on the desk "—and if you ever acted with a high hand, now is the time. Call in the Space Patrol fleet, and radio for the War Fleet. Declare war on Venus if they won't cooperate. But get those fellows and that second ship!"

Orson picked up the notebook and stuffed it in his pocket. "I'll tear Venus apart," he said savagely. "I'll get every last one of them; and no other detonator ship will leave Venus, you can bank on that. But, Martin, what about Kathleen—and Coleridge?"

Martin Brand stared blankly at Orson. "Kathleen?" he asked. "What about her? And who's Coleridge?"

"You...don't know?" faltered Orson.

A peculiar expression crossed Brand's face. "I don't know a thing," he said. "Out with it, man. What's on your mind?"

"You mean you, a member of the fifth-column group, didn't know that we had another SS man in the group? His Venusian name is Forsythe…"

Brand's face went pasty. "Forsythe…" he whispered. "Did you say Forsythe?"

Orson didn't answer. He saw in Brand's face that there was no need.

"So *that's* what bothered me when I saw her walk away from me…" said Brand in stunned tones. "How could I have failed to recognize the swing of those proud shoulders…?" His voice failed and he stood as though stricken with vocal paralysis.

"Martin," said Orson. "What's wrong…?"

Slowly Martin Brand drew in his breath, then he sighed in a great shuddering gust. His face took on a set of utter pain and despair. "She's been executed," he said in almost unrecognizable tones. "Forsythe was detected by Lieutenant Farrow. Farrow knew all about him, and carried out a plan to trap Forsythe and the new operative he was bringing in. I never suspected who it was. I didn't recognize her, even when I was picked to question her before the fake arrest you fellows pulled. She fooled me both ways—I thought she was just a Venusian trollop…"

He whirled on Orson. "Why'd she come here?" he asked. "Nobody back on Earth would have sent her where I was. It would have been too dangerous to me, now that I was the key man here. *How* could she have come?"

"It was all her idea," said Orson hoarsely. "All along she kept insisting you weren't dead, and finally she made up her mind to find out. She told me she was going to open your coffin and find out if you were really there. There was no talking her out of it, so I did the next best thing; I went with her. Naturally your body wasn't in the coffin."

"She figured Venus was the only place you could have gone, and that you were still working for the SS or you'd have contacted me or her. So, without telling me, she took her own private ship to Venus.

"I went to Senator Beasley and made a clean breast of the whole matter—which was hardly necessary; they had both of us ticketed already, from our fingerprints in the tomb. It wound up with me going to Venus on this job, a fake story about your body being recovered, and my own execution so I could come here without suspicion.

"That's the whole story…" Orson stopped speaking.

Brand's face had become stony. "Kathy was always that way," he said emotionlessly. "She had three strikes against her the minute she fell in love with me. I'm death to everybody I come near, but this'll be the last time. This time it's 'suicide' Martin Brand for sure—because that's what blowing up the detonator ship will be, for me. Without Kathy, I don't want to go any further…"

He thrust out his hand and Orson took it wordlessly. "So long, Hal. Get those babies for me, will you? You can be sure I'll take care of my end of the job. Kathy never shirked her duty when she saw it. The least I can do is finish her job off the way she would have."

Orson swallowed hard as he said, "Goodbye, Martin. Don't worry about my end of it. Venus will be scoured clean of these vermin within twenty-four hours, and if I can get hold of that fellow Farrow, I'll skin him inch by inch and layer by layer."

"That's part of my job," said Brand. "He'll be on the big ship with me. Only thing I'll regret is dirtying up Space with his atoms."

One long instant both men looked at each other levelly, then Brand spun on his heel and almost ran from the room.

Hal Orson swore and snatched up his desk phone.

# CHAPTER FOURTEEN

The ceaseless drip of water from the dark green leaves of the lush vegetation in the Venusian jungle formed a whispering background for the *slosh-slosh* of Kathleen's feet through the mud as she stumbled along ahead of Don Coleridge. Behind Coleridge came Farrow, his handsome face still sardonic and gloating. During the two hours he had urged them along the muddy trail, there had been no chance for escape. Farrow was as alert as a fox, and his finger was constantly on the trigger of his steam gun.

Now his voice barked out. "Stop. This is where we get off."

Kathleen halted, but did not turn around. She stood hopelessly, looking at the leafy jungle all around her. Coleridge, however, turned on Farrow heavily.

"You'd better get me the first shot, Farrow," he said. "Because I'm going to kill you if you don't. Once these fingers wrap your neck, it'll take more than a steam gun to get me loose."

Farrow laughed. "Heroics, eh?" he sneered. "Tell you what I'll do—I'll give you a fighting chance. I'll toss my other steam gun at your feet. If you can pick it up and fire it before you're dead, you might even hit me, who knows?"

"You haven't that much sporting blood in you," exploded Coleridge.

"No?" asked Farrow. "Well, start jumping, friend. *Here's the gun.*" With a swift motion he drew his second steam gun from its holster and tossed it toward Coleridge. He waited until Coleridge's fingers had closed on the gun.

Coleridge stretched himself out full length in the mud. Like lightning he snatched the gun. Without trying to get up, he leveled it and pressed the trigger. Nothing happened.

Farrow laughed contemptuously. "Only an Earthman would be idiot enough even to consider the possibility that anyone would risk his life on that sort of sporting deal." With a sneer he pressed the trigger of his steam gun and Coleridge shuddered once, then lay still.

Kathleen, who had faced the two when the conversation had begun, looked at Farrow calmly, repressing a shudder with every ounce of her self control.

"Do you need to shoot me?" she asked.

Farrow lifted his eyebrows. "That's an odd question," he said. "Why do you put it that way?"

"Because maybe you've made a mistake."

"I never make mistakes."

"You've ascertained positively that I was working with him?" she asked.

He looked at her a moment. "I see what you mean. Well, does it make any difference?"

"Not any more," she said bitterly. "It might have, back at the cafe Venus de Milo."

"Just what difference might it have made?" There was a slight frown on his face.

She shrugged. "I was watching you..." She let her voice trail off.

Farrow stared at her thoughtfully for a moment. "That's true," he said, a peculiar light in his eyes. "You were looking at me a great deal." He was still an instant longer, then he said bluntly. "Why?"

She looked at the ground and answered, "Why does a woman look at a man?"

"Maybe in this case because she was a spy," he suggested.

"That's why I said it didn't make any difference now," she said. "Go ahead; get it over with. I can see you'll follow your orders regardless…"

His jaw tightened a bit and a flush of anger began to creep up from his neck. "I'm not exactly the flunky you think I am," he snapped. "I don't follow orders, I give them."

Kathleen felt a slow surge of hope rise within her. "In this case you are following them," she said. "Your boss, the Martian, ordered you to kill me. Neither he nor you know whether I'm a spy or not, but that seems to make no difference. Coleridge butted into my life, and now I'm going to pay for it…" She looked at the body on the ground and her eyes blazed for a moment, then they dulled again and the hopeless tone crept back into her voice. "Besides, it's too late…"

Farrow began walking slowly toward her, a strange light in his eyes. His gaze was devouring her figure, appraising her again and again. He jammed the steam gun into her stomach and held it there, his finger on the trigger.

"Nobody's giving me orders," he said. "I do things because I want to, and when I want to do a thing, I do it. That fat Martian back there means nothing to me—except that my position now assures me of at least a governorship back on Earth when we take over—and that'll be very soon now. As a matter of fact, I'll be one of the few top Venusians on Earth. Not even the old Earth Romans will be able to hold a candle to the spot I'll be in."

"If you're trying to torture me, you can forget about it," she blazed at him. "What difference does it make to me whether your position on Earth is better than an Emperor's? Go ahead and kill me. Follow out your orders and get it over with."

"I don't follow orders," he repeated. "I give them." He pressed the gun more firmly against her and moved closer. "For instance, kiss me…"

She looked up at him. She tossed her hair back with a defiant gesture. "Why not?" she said. "I was thinking of it back at the Venus de Milo—when it might have meant something…"

She flung her arms around his neck and placed her lips against his. She kissed him passionately once, then dropped her arms and looked down. Her face flushed, and she held her breath tightly to make it grow even more so. "Now go ahead and kill me," she said.

For reply he laughed. "I'm giving the orders, not you. Here, help me toss this body into the quicksand." He sheathed his gun and waited.

Kathleen looked at him, then looked at the crumpled body of Don Coleridge. "It'll be a pleasure," she said.

When they had dragged the body off the trail and shoved it into the quicksand bog just beyond its edge, they stood watching the body sink slowly out of sight. Farrow looked at Kathleen a long moment.

"One thing I'm sure of," he said.

"What's that?"

"You aren't a spy, but you *are* my kind of woman."

"I don't know how you're going to manage it," she said, "but if you do, you won't regret it."

He licked his lips. "I'll manage it," he said, "and come to think of it, you *will* make a lovely Empress."


The ponderous power of the giant, atom-propelled Martian warship shoved her through the void like a giant fist, aimed directly at the Earth. Behind lay Venus, a giant white ball in space, already several million miles astern.

Martin Brand stared back at it through the portholes of the belly deck and shook his head. He bit his lip savagely and turned away from the white planet almost angrily. His face was grim and drawn. With an effort he thrust down the vision of a proud Irish face surrounded by a cloud of turbulent red hair, and curiously superimposed over it the slant eyes and pale green complexion of a Venusian girl.

"She did her job," he whispered. "Now it's up to me to do mine."

He made his way slowly toward midship and finally came to the bomb section. Here, on networks of steel rails, rested the atomic bomb armament of the ship, ready to be launched in rocket warheads. There were hundreds of them here, capable of devastating the cities of a whole planet, once they could be launched from a range where accurate aim was possible. These would be the bombs with which this and other, but smaller Martian ships would finish up operations on remaining Earth centers of resistance, once the giant detonator generators located in the bow of the ship sent out the fatal impulse that would make raging atomic infernos of hundreds of strategic areas on Earth.

When that impulse went out, the death blow to Earth's resistance would have been dealt. No matter how many Martian battleships, converging on Earth after the big blast, were destroyed by Earth's mighty space navy, it would be meaningless, with no further bases of supply for that navy. Once out of fuel, they would be drifting hulks at the mercy of the enemy. And Mars, right now, was on the other side of the sun, too far away for successful counter-attack.

Brand looked at the atomic arsenal before him, gazed calculatingly at the bomb bays through which the rockets would dart when launched and nodded grimly. Before him rose the vision of a battleship almost as big as this one, inside the Black Hole on Luna. Once more he heard Estelle

Carter's voice ringing in its madness in his ears as he crept closer to the belly of her ship. He lived again the gigantic flash that marked the detonation of her bombs, exploded by his atomic barrage from the lone rifle in his stolen cruiser. These big ships were amazingly vulnerable, provided they could be approached. Out in space this was impossible, but in the Black Hole it had been easy—just as it would be comparatively easy to do it here. He would merely launch himself into space in the auxiliary cruiser, and fire the instant he cleared the ship and could bring the bomb bays into line. He would have at most a minute or two, before the automatic radar-operated guns would blow his cruiser to bits.

Either way, it was the end for Martin Brand. He didn't intend to take any chances on being hit before he could explode those bombs. Given three minutes, he might stand a chance to get away, but he didn't intend to take those three minutes.

Carefully he considered his chances. On this giant battleship were less than fifty men. Almost all of the great ship was robot-controlled. In space warfare, little was risked in the way of manpower. Also, in automatic operation there was almost no chance of such failure as might occur from the human element. Accordingly, Brand could make his way about the giant ship with little chance of meeting another of the crew. Since the take-off, he had observed carefully just what and where each man's duties were. He was satisfied that he knew the time schedule of every man in this section of the ship.

He glanced at his watch. In one hour he would make the attempt.

As he thought of it, he felt cold.

# CHAPTER FIFTEEN

"All right, you can come out now."

Farrow released the catch on the ventilated container and lifted the cover. With one hand he helped Kathleen clamber out of her hiding place in the storage hold of the ship. Then he stepped back and stared at her as she straightened her rumpled clothes and brushed out her hair as best she could with her fingers.

"You look beautiful even in the morning," he observed. "If you look that good coming out of a packing box, you really ought to be a sensation coming out of swan's down and silk."

"Where are we?" asked Kathleen, advancing toward him and nestling against his shoulder.

"Out in space."

"I know that," she pouted. She slid her arms around his neck and kissed him.

He pushed her away. "I'd better answer your question first," he said. "That is, if you're really interested."

She shrugged. "It doesn't make much difference. But I would like to know how long I'm going to be cooped up here."

"We'll be landing on Luna, which will be surrendered to us just as soon as they realize what's happened to Earth, in about two Earth days. And when we land, you'll come off this ship like you came on—in that box. Once you're off, you'll be a free woman, and I'll pick you up when I've finished my work. After that..."

"Your assignment to an Earth area as governor!" she exclaimed. "What area do you think you'll get?"

"I've expressed a preference for the United States area," he said. "And, quite frankly, they could hardly give me less. I rank second only to Captain Lutain."

"Who's he?" asked Kathleen petulantly. "Why should you rank second to anybody?"

Farrow reached out and pulled her to him. "Maybe you've got something there," he said admiringly. "Why should I? I think something may be done about that, but don't worry about it. Right now, how about continuing that kiss where you left off? We've got about an hour before I've got to be back at my station."

"Nobody will bother us here?"

He grinned. "Nobody."

Kathleen glanced around the storage hold. "Isn't there anything to drink in this place?" she complained. "Ought to be something here…"

Farrow lifted his eyebrows. "Say, baby, maybe there is at that. As a matter of fact, the Martian has a stock of the best brought along with him wherever he goes. Maybe it's here."

He walked up and down the storage racks, and finally exclaimed in pleasure. "Here it is." He ripped open a carton and produced a bottle. Kathleen came to his side, took it and kissed him. "Better take another one," she suggested, "we might need it."

As Farrow turned to get another bottle, she raised her own above his head and brought it down with all her might. Without a sound Lieutenant Farrow slid to the floor.

Working swiftly, Kathleen tore his clothes into strips and bound him tightly. When she had finished, she surveyed her work with satisfaction. He would not escape from those bonds unless somebody released him. They had been applied with true SS efficiency.

Picking up Farrow's two steam guns, Kathleen turned and made her way toward the door of the storage hull.

Martin Brand made a final instrument adjustment in the electronics' systems room, which was in his charge. He hoped that the slight reduction in power output he had made would slow up the action of the radar-operated guns. This would give him perhaps three or four minutes more of valuable time, in case he encountered difficulty in lining up his guns with the bomb bay openings on this heavily armored ship, a hit on the outer hull would be worse than useless with such a small rifle. Only a direct hit on the bombs would do the trick.

Now, his lips pressed tightly together, Brand made his way down decks toward the launching level for the tiny cruisers the battleship carried. In a few more minutes he would step into one of them, press the button that set the launching mechanism into operation, and would be hurled into space. Once he was out, a quick burst of the rockets, and a speedy dive and loop ought to bring him up with his bow gun pointing directly at his target. He knew he would get time for only one pass at the bomb bays, or at the outside, one more desperate loop at six gravities. He hoped he could hold his senses long enough, in that event, to press the firing lever at the proper instant.

"I'll get 'em the *first* time..." he muttered.

He made his way without incident past the two operations decks. On deck three he almost ran into a Venusian. He saluted sharply and went on. The man also saluted and went on his way.

He reached the launching deck without seeing anyone else. Quickly he approached the bulkhead door beyond which the cruisers lay. As he neared it, there came a hoarse shout down the long corridor that led to the storage deck. There came the bright flash of a steam gun and a horrid scream of a man in agony. Two more bright flashes illuminated the corridor, and then came the sound of running feet.

Brand raced desperately for the bulkhead door. He had to get through it and get it closed before those running feet, whatever they meant, came into sight. He cursed the luck that had caused such an unexpected commotion. He had no time to wonder what it was, but steam gun in hand he was racing directly toward those bright flashes.

All at once a racing figure hurled itself into view at the end of the corridor. Suddenly it slid to a halt, dropped to a knee, and leveled a steam gun. Unable to halt his headlong dash in time to aim his own weapon, Brand dove for the floor.

A beam crackled over his prostrate body, and hot metal flew from the wall behind him. Instantly Brand was on his knees, aiming his own gun at the figure down the corridor. The newcomer was now erect, taking aim at him, Brand's eyes widened and he dropped his gun in stark astonishment.

*"Kathleen!"* he bellowed, and again hurled his body away from her bolt. Once more she missed and he yelled again. "Kathy, Kathy! It's me—Martin Brand! Don't shoot!"

The figure down the corridor stood stock still for an instant, then slumped to the floor.

Brand leaped to his feet and raced to her side. With one single motion he swept her into his arms and raced back to the bulkhead door leading to the cruisers. He kicked it open, leaped through, and laid Kathleen down on the floor. He shut the door, bolted it securely, and then picked Kathleen up again. He carried her to the nearest cruiser, locked in its launching ways, and thrust her inside. In an instant he had released the locking mechanism and clambered inside himself.

It took only a few seconds to thrust Kathleen into a shock seat and strap her in. Then he raced for the pilot seat.

He ignored the straps, using only the support bar to hold him fast. Frantically he pressed the starting button, and as soon as the force of the launching acceleration told him the ship was moving toward the exit port, which was opening slowly, he jabbed the rocket lever forward.

Red flame filled the cruiser compartment, and the ship leaped forward like a live thing. It roared out of the exit port before it was even wholly opened, and Brand reeled under a savage shock as the ship smashed the doors outward. But he exulted, because if he failed at his first pass it would be impossible to open the bulkhead door. There'd be no firing at him from the other ships in their cradles.

He hurled the ship into a steep dive, and brought it up tightly in an inside loop. Streaks of white filled the blackness of space. They were the stars passing before his eyes in dizzy passage. The battleship was nowhere in sight, and he strained his eyes to pick it up as he continued around the killing loop. Blackness threatened to sweep over his vision before it suddenly loomed over him. Then, all at once, he was bearing directly for it, and there in the forepart of the hull were the black openings of the rocket-bomb bays.

Brand pressed the firing studs of the cruiser's bow atomic rifles, and locked them into position. For an agonizing three seconds he bore straight for the openings, then he looped over again, at maximum speed. The blackness before his eyes swept over him like a tide, but all at once it seemed to recede for an instant under an intolerable brilliance. Then it surged up again and this time overwhelmed him. As it did so, his leaden hand pulled the steering lever into neutral...

## CHAPTER SIXTEEN

The taste in his mouth was salty. It was also warm, and he wondered vaguely why. Then he realized his nose was bleeding profusely. All at once someone swabbed at his face with a large piece of cotton.

"Sissy," he heard a voice say.

He kept his eyes closed, trying to remember something. Then it came to him, slowly, like a movie in slow motion... Kathy's face, racing toward him; white bolts of her steam gun darting at him; whirling action; her body heavy in his arms; the roar of the cruiser rockets; red flame; black space; spinning stars; an ugly, growing black tide over his eyes; a brilliant white flash; blackness, into which her face grew above him... He realized that he was opening his eyes. Her face remained before him...a Venusian face, slant-eyed, tear-streaked, nose bloody.

"It's a new face," he said. "Fooled me, but I should have known that walk..."

"So that's what you were looking at?"

He nodded. "You won't ever be able to hide that gait," he grinned. "It's as Irish as the Sweepstakes."

"You fooled me too. How I failed to recognize the uppity self-pity of Martin Brand, though, I'll never know..."

"It's not pity," he retorted, struggling erect to discover himself on the floor beside the pilot seat of the cruiser. "You women seem to have a penchant for showing a man the flat of your back."

"You're not looking at my back now," she said.

He looked at her a long moment. "And I'm never going to," he said, "but where are we? What happened?"

"You blew the battleship up, just like you did the Martian fleet inside the Black Hole."

"So you admit, finally, that I did blow it up?" he demanded. "But let me at that radio—we've got to get a pickup before we get clean out of the solar system..."

She pushed him back firmly. "No you don't. I've tried to get you where I've got you for eleven years, and now that we're alone with no chance of being interrupted, I'm not going to let you radio to anybody. We don't need any help.

I've got this ship pointed in an orbit that will bring us to Earth's atmosphere in about forty-eight hours."

"Forty-eight hours? How far are we from Earth?"

"About three thousand miles."

"But that's only two hours away," he said, struggling once more to get up. She pushed him back again.

"Martin Brand, that may be your idea of how to travel, but it's going to take forty-eight hours if I have to *back* this ship up to do it. And besides…"

"Besides what?"

"If you don't wipe that blood off your face, I'm going to kiss you anyway."

He looked up at her and grinned. "Go ahead," he said. "And while you're doing that, I'll try to imagine that's green lipstick on *your* face—sissy!"

A minute later he pulled away frantically, gasping. "I've got to breathe," he panted. "How many G's do you think a guy can take…?"

"I'll tell you—forty-eight hours from now," she said sweetly. "Draw a deep breath—here I come again."

Outside the portholes, the green earth rotated slowly beneath the drifting ship.

## THE END

*If you've enjoyed this book, you will not want to miss these terrific titles…*

## ARMCHAIR SCI-FI & HORROR DOUBLE NOVELS, $12.95 each

**D-71**  **THE DEEP END** by Gregory Luce
**TO WATCH BY NIGHT** by Robert Moore Williams

**D-72**  **SWORDSMAN OF LOST TERRA** by Poul Anderson
**PLANET OF GHOSTS** by David V. Reed

**D-73**  **MOON OF BATTLE** by J. J. Allerton
**THE MUTANT WEAPON** by Murray Leinster

**D-74**  **OLD SPACEMEN NEVER DIE!** John Jakes
**RETURN TO EARTH** by Bryan Berry

**D-75**  **THE THING FROM UNDERNEATH** by Milton Lesser
**OPERATION INTERSTELLAR** by George O. Smith

**D-76**  **THE BURNING WORLD** by Algis Budrys
**FOREVER IS TOO LONG** by Chester S. Geier

**D-77**  **THE COSMIC JUNKMAN** by Rog Phillips
**THE ULTIMATE WEAPON** by John W. Campbell

**D-78**  **THE TIES OF EARTH** by James H. Schmitz
**CUE FOR QUIET** by Thomas L. Sherred

**D-79**  **SECRET OF THE MARTIANS** by Paul W. Fairman
**THE VARIABLE MAN** by Philip K. Dick

**D-80**  **THE GREEN GIRL** by Jack Williamson
**THE ROBOT PERIL** by Don Wilcox

## ARMCHAIR SCIENCE FICTION CLASSICS, $12.95 each

**C-25**  **THE STAR KINGS**
by Edmond Hamilton

**C-26**  **NOT IN SOLITUDE**
by Kenneth Gantz

**C-32**  **PROMETHEUS II**
by S. J. Byrne

## ARMCHAIR SCIENCE FICTION & HORROR GEMS SERIES, $12.95 each

**G-7**  **SCIENCE FICTION GEMS, Vol. Four**
Jack Sharkey and others

**G-8**  **HORROR GEMS, Vol. Four**
Seabury Quinn and others

*If you've enjoyed this book, you will not want to miss these terrific titles…*

## ARMCHAIR SCI-FI, FANTASY, & HORROR DOUBLE NOVELS, $12.95 each

**D-81**   **THE LAST PLEA** by Robert Bloch
**THE STATUS CIVILIZATION** by Robert Sheckley

**D-82**   **WOMAN FROM ANOTHER PLANET** by Frank Belknap Long
**HOMECALLING** by Judith Merril

**D-83**   **WHEN TWO WORLDS MEET** by Robert Moore Williams
**THE MAN WHO HAD NO BRAINS** by Jeff Sutton

**D-84**   **THE SPECTRE OF SUICIDE SWAMP** by E. K. Jarvis
**IT'S MAGIC, YOU DOPE!** by Jack Sharkey

**D-85**   **THE STARSHIP FROM SIRIUS** by Rog Phillips
**FINAL WEAPON** by Everett Cole

**D-86**   **TREASURE ON THUNDER MOON** by Edmond Hamilton
**TRAIL OF THE ASTROGAR** by Henry Haase

**D-87**   **THE VENUS ENIGMA** by Joe Gibson
**THE WOMAN IN SKIN 13** by Paul W. Fairman

**D-88**   **THE MAD ROBOT** by William P. McGivern
**THE RUNNING MAN** by J. Holly Hunter

**D-89**   **VENGEANCE OF KYVOR** by Randall Garrett
**AT THE EARTH'S CORE** by Edgar Rice Burroughs

**D-90**   **DWELLERS OF THE DEEP** by Don Wilcox
**NIGHT OF THE LONG KNIVES** by Fritz Leiber

## ARMCHAIR SCIENCE FICTION CLASSICS, $12.95 each

**C-28**   **THE MAN FROM TOMORROW**
by Stanton A. Coblentz

**C-29**   **THE GREEN MAN OF GRAYPEC**
by Festus Pragnell

**C-30**   **THE SHAVER MYSTERY, Book Four**
by Richard S. Shaver

## ARMCHAIR MASTERS OF SCIENCE FICTION SERIES, $16.95 each

**MS-7**   **MASTERS OF SCIENCE FICTION AND FANTASY, Vol. Seven**
Lester del Rey, "The Band Played On" and other tales

**MS-8**   **MASTERS OF SCIENCE FICTION, Vol. Eight**
Milton Lesser, "'A' as in Android" and other tales

# THEIR COMING SPELLED DOOM FOR MANKIND!

This was no ordinary dream—it was a nightmare! For when Clark Dane woke he didn't know where he was or how he had come to be there. Nor could he remember anything about his past. He was also under guard…and under arrest for supposedly being a Kalquoi spy! The Kalquoi were shape-changing aliens who could masquerade as humans and were slowly taking over the galaxy, destroying everything that stood in their path. Now with the last of the human race in danger, Dane needed to find answers about his past, answers that would hopefully help him save the future of mankind. When Nelva Guthrie offered help, Dane found a strong and surprising ally. Together they searched for answers and a way to stop the Kalquoi, but the answers they found weren't exactly what they expected!

# ABOUT DWIGHT V. SWAIN

Dwight Vreeland Swain was born November 17, 1915 to John Edgar Swain, a railroad telegrapher, and Florence Marietta Vreeland. Growing up in Rochester, MI, he showed early promise as a writer, selling non-fiction to a Sunday school paper while in high school. He got his BA in journalism at the University of Michigan in 1937, then started working as a newspaperman and editor. He held a wide variety of other jobs, including doing door-to-door sales; working as an ordinary seaman; acting as a press agent for a mind reader, and interviewing murderers for true crime books. Over the next twenty years, he sold over a million words of pulp fiction—mostly space opera novels in magazines like *Imagination, Amazing Stories,* and *Fantastic Adventures*. Swain wrote many of these novels after carefully studying previously commissioned illustrations. Famed author Robert Silverberg once described Swain as "a lively man and a very skillful pulp storyteller." His many hobbies included the harmonica, the violin, swimming, traveling, archaeology, sociology, psychology, reading, and economics. Dwight V. Swain passed away on February 24, 1992.

# BRING BACK MY BRAIN!

By
DWIGHT V. SWAIN

ARMCHAIR FICTION
PO Box 4369, Medford, Oregon   97501-0168

# CHAPTER ONE

IT WAS A WORLD without a past or future; a shining shadow-world borne of sheer madness, a thousand echoing eternities beyond all space and time.

Now the pulsing radiance grew brighter—so bright it sent pain-tipped needles stabbing through Clark Dane's brain. He writhed under its relentless, throbbing pressure; tried to draw back, to cry out.

But the strange lethargy still clung to him, all-encumbering as a leaden pall. As in a nightmare, he lay prostrate, paralyzed, unable to move or speak.

Numbly, he wondered if he were dead.

Only then the silent laughter rose again—taunting; chilling—and he knew that life still stirred within him.

The face came with the laughter, floating through the swirling radiance as a shadow drifts through fog. Hollow-cheeked, hollow-eyed, hairless as a sand-scoured, tide-washed skull, it hovered before Dane like a living death's-head, closer than ever before.

Where previously had he known this Being-Without-A-Name, Dane wondered? What malicious trick of circumstance had brought the two of them together?

Only those were things somehow beyond his powers of recall at the moment; questions that, strangely, seemed to find no answers within his aching brain.

Shuddering, he squeezed the eyes of his mind tight shut against the spectre.

But the face would not go away. Smirking, sardonic, evil, deep-lined with old sins, it hung motionless now, as if mocking Dane in his torment while it reiterated its eternal theme: "I am your master, slave! Bow down! Bow down to your creator! Acknowledge your serfdom here and now!"

In spite of himself, Dane cringed.

"Say it, you fool! Say you are my slave!"

"No, damn you! Never; not ever…"

"You dare not deny me! You know it!" The malevolent eyes in the death's-head skull gleamed hot and bright as fire-jewels—probing, penetrating, skewering to the core of Dane's very brain. "Say it, I tell you! Say you are my slave!"

Dane's jaws ached with pressure. Desperately, he tried to fight the nightmare image from his mind.

"Acknowledge me, slave! I am your master!"

Dane's senses reeled. He was panting now. "I—I—"

"Say it!"

"I—am—your slave…"

Thin, cruel lips peeled back from stained teeth in a grimace of sadistic triumph. The soundless, soulless laughter rang forth louder than ever.

Dane sobbed aloud.

As if his reaction were a signal, the mocking face began to fade, back into the eddying radiance from whence it came. Where it had hung, a new shape rose.

Inanimate, this one; yet clean-cut and graceful as any living thing. Slim, silvery, needle-sharp, it poised like a gigantic lance flung skyward from its squat, buttressed base.

Dane's raw nerves calmed a fraction. The dream-pain ebbed away. Fascinated, he studied the shining shaft.

For even as he first glimpsed it, he knew in a rush that his life, his fate, his very being, somehow were linked tight to it. Completely strange to him, it yet held intangible elements of familiarity beyond all ordinary knowledge.

Now the shaft seemed to drift closer, just as had the face before it, and Dane saw that a vertical slot ran almost its full length, from top to bottom, like a vastly elongated needle-eye.

Slowly, while Dane watched, the shaft turned above its base. A second slot appeared, precisely like the first. Then a third. Through the openings, Dane glimpsed a maze of coils and wiring.

Frowning in spite of himself, he glanced down at the base, then stiffened.

For the shaft hung completely free in the air as if invisibly suspended from above, well clear of the metal-rimmed socket in its bed-plate!

A chill ran through Dane. Yet he could not tear his eyes away from the shining needle. It was almost as if another unheard voice, soundless as that of the vanished face, were hammering thoughts into his brain: "Heed well, Clark Dane! Let no detail escape you, lest the lack of it shall speed you to your doom! This shaft—it stands as symbol of all your dreams and hopes, your destiny..."

Then thought and image alike were fading; the lace and its mind-voice back once more: "Remember, slave, I am your master, now and always! Dare to challenge me again and instant death shall be your doom!"

Never had the hollow eyes gleamed with such menace. Never had the bony, hairless face been etched more deeply with lines that spoke of ruthlessness and iniquity.

Slowly, reluctantly, Dane bowed his head. "I am your slave. You are my master."

But deep within him another voice was speaking in a savage, sullen whisper, so low as not even to reach the frontal lobes of his brain: "No! I'm not your slave! No man's my master! And some day, no matter what you threaten—some day, we'll see who dies!

## CHAPTER TWO

AT FIRST IT SEEMED to Dane that he was racing through space, hurtling out in a whirling, swirling arc that left the whole solar system far behind. The stars, the galaxies, fell into chaos in his wake. New nebulae spread out before him, unseen by living eye until his advent.

Awestruck, unable even to breathe, he could only stare at it all in unnerved wonder.

Then, slowly, that stage passed. Little by little, the void about him took on substance, until at last he found himself swimming somewhere far beneath the surface of a viscid sea…fighting his way upward through the horror of dark, chimera-teeming depths inches at a time in that agonizing, snail-slow progression known only in the world of dreams.

But there came a moment when even swimming demanded too much effort. He floated, limp, rising slowly towards the daylight miles above him, free to the whim of every changing eddy of a foam flecked, pale-green sea.

As from afar, then, a voice reached him dimly—a real voice, this time; one that spoke words aloud and face to face instead of only in the mind.

A woman's voice, surprisingly.

"I want him at the Record Center as fast as I can get him here," the voice said firmly. "That's why I'm coming out from Mars to make the pickup. There hasn't been a genuine case of amnesia reported from any of the inner planets in over a hundred years, and I've no intention of letting this one slip by me."

Of a sudden the pale-green sea seemed to separate beneath Dane. It left him stranded on a smooth, level surface, resilient and not too hard.

Cautiously, he moved his fingers over it, recognized the texture of heavy synthetic kalor.

A bed, then.

The woman's voice went on, brisk and businesslike yet somehow intense: "I can't impress all of you too much with how important it is not to upset this man. Any shock prior to the complete celloscopic and hypnoanalytic examination we'll give him here might do untold damage—both to him, and to our chance of successfully working through his case."

Very carefully, Dane opened his eyes.

He looked out upon a dully glittering expanse of green telonium spaceship bulkhead. The viewing plate of a built-in visiscreen occupied a spot directly before him at eye level.

Centered on the plate was the image of the woman who was speaking.

Narrow-eyed, Dane studied her.

She had turned now to a concise discussion of technical details regarding amnesia—and that made the contrast between her words and her appearance all the more marked. For even over the visiscreen there was no denying her lithe, slender loveliness; and as Dane gazed up at the smooth oval of her face...stared into her cool grey eyes...he could visualize her in almost any role more easily than that of scientist or savant.

If he ever met her, perhaps he could persuade her to play a more feminine part.

It was a pleasant thought. But even as it struck Dane, the woman broke off. Her soft lips parted in a sudden, half-rueful smile. "I'm talking too much. You've better things to do than listen to my lectures, and—"

THE CLICK of a switch cut her off in mid-sentence. A harsh male voice snarled, "I'll say she talks too much! And for my part, I'm all through listening."

Dane shifted quickly; discovered for the first time that he shared the telonium chamber with three men grouped about a table: two in space-fleet uniform and one—the speaker—without.

The ununiformed man, squat and heavy-bodied, still gripped the visiscreen's remote control switch, his piggish, close-set eyes glazed hard with anger, his broad, lumpy face working.

The pig-eyes flicked to Dane as he turned. The lumpy face split in an ugly grin. "Well! Sleeping beauty's awake! Maybe we can come up with some answers of our own after all, before her royal highness from the Record Center gets here."

The man surged up as he spoke, flexing corded arms thick with coarse black hair. To Dane, he looked to be in his late twenties. His body bulged so heavy with muscle that his half-bald bullet head seemed to grow directly from his shoulders.

But one of the space-fleet officers rose too. "Hold it, Pfaff!" he rapped. "Nelva Guthrie's given us our orders—and whether you like it or not, she's supervisor of the whole Mars Record Center. In a situation like this that gives her the rank to make what she says stick."

"Oh, does it, now?" sneered the man called Pfaff. "Personally, I always thought that where the Kalquoi were concerned, Security outranked anyone."

"The Kalquoi—?" The second space-fleet officer was on his feet now, gesturing. "Slow down a minute on that, Pfaff. What have the Kalquoi got to do with this poor devil?"

"We picked him off an asteroid, didn't we?" the bullet-headed Pfaff slashed back belligerently. "If that doesn't tie him to the Kalquoi, what would it take? They've infiltrated the whole damn belt, and you know it!"

"But just because he was marooned there—"

"Marooned, hell!" Pfaff hammered the butt of a rock-like fist against the doloid table. "Who marooned him, that's what I want to know! No man just pops up on an asteroid, naked as the day he was born, without even a breather mask for company!"

The two officers exchanged helpless glances.

"Answer me, you chitzas!" Pfaff bellowed. Again he smashed his great fist down upon the table. "I want to know who marooned him! And after you've told me that, I want to know who sent out the distress signal on him that we picked up. And who pumped that cave full of air and then slapped an energy seal on it so he'd have something to breathe till we got there. And finally, who"—a momentary pause while he snatched up an object from the table—"who left him this Kalquoi yat-stick to play with?"

"Well—" The first space-fleet officer groped futilely for words.

The second looked away, not speaking.

For a long moment Pfaff watched them—pig eyes aglitter, bullet head drawn far between the massive shoulders.

Then, slowly, his snarl changed to a smirk. He straightened; made a show of smoothing his rumpled short-sleeved, civilian tunic.

"For my money," he announced in a suddenly bland and unctuous voice, "we've got no evidence whatever that this starbo"—a gesture to Dane—"is even human!"

In spite of himself, Dane went rigid. The officers' heads snapped round as if on springs. "What—?"

"You heard me." Pfaff was almost purring now. "The Kalquoi are shape-shifters; you know that. That's what makes them so dangerous. One minute, they'll be obviously alien—crystals floating in mid-air and radiating colored light like so many prisms. The next, one's a rock, another's a tal-string, and the third's bouncing around pretending to be the ball in a byul-game."

A THIN THREAD of irritation began to creep through Dane. Unsteadily, he pulled himself to a sitting position and swung his legs over the edge of his cot. "Wait a minute, there…"

"Shut up, you stabat!" Pfaff threw out the command in the manner of a huecco-trainer addressing a particularly doltish pupil. And then, to the officers once more: "Don't you see? The brain-drain's stopped the Kalquoi cold. But supposing they could masquerade as humans, the way they do inanimate objects! Before we knew it, they'd take over the inner planets, the way they have the outer!"

Dane drew a deep, careful breath. "The only trouble is, I'm not a Kalquoi," he announced firmly.

"Oh." This time Pfaff turned to face him. "Then who are you, may I ask?"

"My name's Clark Dane."

"Clark Dane. Very good." Pfaff licked thick lips, as if enjoying the whole situation. "Now, tell us some other things: where you were born; who your parents were; your work assignment number; occupational classification; residence registration; how and why you came to be on the asteroid where we found you."

"Why, I—" Dane started to speak, then stopped short, groping. "I—I—"

"Yes, yes. Go on." Pfaff was grinning openly now, head thrust forward as he prodded.

A numbness crept through Dane. Desperately he searched the farthest corners of his brain for answers to the other's questions.

Answers that just weren't there.

Pfaff chuckled; goaded: "It couldn't be you don't know, could it? Nor that you can't remember anything about the past except your name?"

Dane didn't answer. Bewilderment; confusion; sheer, stark panic—they roiled within him; put knots in the pit of his stomach and made his head reel till he had to cling to the edge of the cot for fear of falling.

Again Pfaff chuckled. "Maybe I'm being too hard on you, Dane." His mockery seared like acid. "If so, I'll apologize. Just prove to me you're not a Kalquoi; that's all I ask."

"Damn it, Pfaff!" the officer nearest to Dane exploded. "You heard what Nelva Guthrie said: any shock's liable to tie this man up permanently. Quit plaguing him!"

Pfaff's air of mock cordiality fell away like a discarded mask. "Is that an order, lieutenant?" he demanded belligerently. "Are you telling me what I can and can't do?"

The other's lips drew tight. "Now wait a minute, Pfaff—"

"No! You wait!" Pfaff thrust his bullet head forward, close to the officer's face. "This is a matter of principle, mister. We'll settle it right now. I'm Security rep on this ship, and I say this Clark Dane pickup's a Security matter. Are you going to contradict me?"

"If need be." The lieutenant's cheeks flamed. "It so happens, Mr. Pfaff, that you've pushed your luck a little too far. Security rep or not, you're overstepping your authority, and I'm not about to stand for it. If need be, I'll take it clear to the captain."

"Well! So it's out in the open at last!" Pig eyes glittering, thick lips twisted in an ugly grin, Pfaff moved in even closer. "You've got a good idea there, too—that business of taking all this to the captain. We'll do it. And then, after that, we'll carry it another step, to a friend of mine. You may have heard of him. His name's Thorburg Jessup."

"Thorburg Jessup—!" The lieutenant's nostrils flared. His eyes distended.

Then, of a sudden, the angry color was draining from his face. Uncertainly, he fell back a step. "Now wait a minute, Pfaff—"

IT WAS AS IF the other hadn't even heard him. "Did you think you were going to get away with it, lieutenant? Did you really?" The Security rep exploded in a roar of contemptuous, scorn-ringing laughter. "Let me tell you something, mister. The blocked-promotion stations are full of brass-braided jackasses who thought they could lock horns with Security reps. Because the minute an officer talks back or pokes his nose into Security business, the rep calls Jessup—and that's the end of the trouble *and* the officer."

For a long, taut moment, then, the silence echoed; a leaden silence, heavy with tension.

"Well, lieutenant?" Pfaff cocked his head. "Which is it going to be? Do you shut up—or do I call Thorburg Jessup?"

The spaceship officer seemed to stop breathing. Then, abruptly, he pivoted and, wordless, stalked from the room.

Not speaking, Pfaff turned his cold, unblinking stare upon the second officer.

The man's gaze faltered; fell. He followed his fellow from the chamber.

Now Pfaff swung round to face Dane, lumpy features aglow with unholy triumph. Slowly, contemplatively, he scrubbed a meaty palm back and forth through the coarse black hair that matted the opposite forearm.

It made a whispering, scratching sort of sound that rasped Dane's nerves worse than all the earlier verbal pyrotechnics. Uneasily, he shifted; swallowed.

Because strive as he might, he still couldn't remember. Not anything.

The realization brought with it a feeling more frightening than anything he'd ever known. It was as if the world—his private world—had vanished, leaving him cast adrift in space blindfolded, without landmarks or triangulation points, all orientation lost.

The sense of helplessness that came with it was almost more than he could bear. Sheer lack of knowledge half-paralyzed him. Desperately, he wondered what he should do; how his role and true identity called for him to react.

Still gloating, Pfaff leaned back; rested his heavy hams against the doloid table. "Well, bucko?" he prodded.

With an effort, Dane held his voice steady. "I can't tell you what I don't know. All those questions—I simply don't remember."

"Nor this thing? You don't remember it, either?"

As he spoke, the Security rep picked up the Kalquoi yatstick from the table and held it out for Dane's inspection.

Frowning, Dane studied it. A good foot long, Earth measurement, and purplish in hue, it was formed of some heavy alien metal. The basic outline was that of a slingshot crotch—a sort of handle that forked into two prongs to form a Y. But a bar across the top closed the fork, and a continuation of the handle came up to meet the bar at right angles, making a T. Bracing members from the point where the stem of the T met the crosspiece ran to the middle of each arm of the Y, then in their turn were joined into a triangle by another crosspiece.

With a little imagination, Dane saw, it would be easy enough to vision the unit in its entirety as forming a word or syllable, YAT.

"It's a funny thing," Pfaff observed with an emphasis anything but mirthful. "No one knows just what these gadgets are for. The best the extraterrestrial ethnologists can come up with is a lot of thes-gas about symbolism and religious significance. That stuff I wouldn't know about. But one thing's for sure: where you find yat-sticks, you find Kalquoi."

Dane made no comment.

"This one," Pfaff pressed, extending the yat-stick, "was lying half under you in that cave where we picked you up."

Dane shrugged.

"That's all you've got to say? You won't tell me any more about it?"

"What can I tell you?" Dane came back wearily. "Don't you understand? I don't know. I can't remember."

The Security rep's broad face drew into a chill, expressionless mask. His bullet head sank deeper between his shoulders.

"All right," he clipped harshly, flinging the yat-stick back down upon the table. "You want it hard, I'll give it to you that way. This is a survey ship. Start talking, or I'll have 'em throw you in the bem-tank."

"The bem-tank—?" Dane stared.

"Don't give me that! You know what I mean! Survey ships bring in samples of extraterrestrial life—the kind of bug-eyed monsters that give a man nightmares even to think about. What they do to you if they get the chance shouldn't happen to a quontab."

A chill ran through Dane. "But I don't know—"

"Tell it to the bems!" Already, Pfaff was jamming his thumb down on a buzzer button. "You had your chance, you stabat! Now we'll play it my way. You and the narcoanalyst and that vidal Nelva Guthrie—you'll see who's got the answers!"

Dane's panic was like a light-lance beam twisting in his midriff. "Please...I..." he choked. "Please..."

Pfaff laughed aloud.

DANE STOPPED SHORT in mid-breath. The goading, the mockery, the pig eyes, the harsh voice, the badgering—all these he'd taken.

But the laugh went one step beyond his limit of endurance.

In the fraction of a second his panic turned to roiling, boiling rage.

What did it matter if he didn't know who he was or from whence he came? Why should he care if his past was a blank, his future a question-mark?

Why indeed—so long as for this one moment he had a course to follow!

Such a course as erasing the grin from Pfaff's thick lips, for example.

And after that—well, he'd play the other moments as they came along, without regard for past or future.

Savagely, then, he lunged up from the cot, straight at the still-laughing Pfaff.

For the barest instant the Security rep stood frozen, eyes blank with startlement. Then, with surprising agility for his heavy-bodied bulk, the man tried to twist aside, out of the way of Dane's rush.

His hip hit the doloid table. He stumbled.

Before he could recover, Dane smashed a fist home to the blubbery lips; felt them spurt blood as they crushed against Pfaff's teeth.

The Security rep reeled. Heart surging with fierce elation, Dane followed up, hammering home a rain of blows to head and body alike.

For an instant the other fell back—head down, hairy arms hugged close to protect the bulging belly.

But only for an instant. Then, with a harsh roar, the bullet head came up again. A fist like a maul swept out in a wide arc, bruising Dane's rib cage. Another blow caught his shoulders; rocked him back on his heels.

Desperately, Dane threw himself sidewise, barely clear of the other's lunge, and let fly a rabbit-punch.

It landed solidly, but it was still a waste of effort. Pfaff spun about with no sign that he had even been hit, and once again, lunged for Dane.

Taking advantage of his longer reach, Dane drove in a quick one-two to Pfaff's face, then started to leap back, away from the other's charge.

But this time it was he who forgot the doloid table. Careening against it, he staggered for a moment off balance.

The next instant Pfaff buried a fist in the pit of Dane's belly. Retching, half-paralyzed, Dane lurched backward; slumped to the floor.

A roar of triumph from Pfaff. He launched a kick powered to break a man's back.

With a tremendous heave, Dane writhed clear just in time.

But already the Security man was kicking again—a bruising, thigh-grazing blow that tore a choked cry from Dane's throat. In desperation he rolled back and under the table, hoping against hope to avoid the other's murderous feet.

Cursing, Pfaff heaved at the table, wrenching the nearest leg clear of its anchor bracket. "You chitza!" he panted, "I'll kill you! D'you hear me? I'll kill you!"

He meant it. It showed in every line and corded, bulging muscle. Stark murder gleamed in his tiny, close-set pig eyes…glistened in the flecks of bloody foam at the mouth-corners and in the sweat-greased folds of the contorted face.

Spasmodically, Dane dragged himself to his feet on the far side of the wrenched, warped table.

Panting, Pfaff tried to reach him; then, failing, clawed for the heavy Kalquoi yat-stick that still lay on the slab between them.

With all his might, Dane heaved at the already-sagging table. The yat-stick slid to the floor on his side.

Pfaff hurled himself after it bodily. Jamming him aside, Dane snatched up the stick and swung it in a tight arc, straight for the base of the Security rep's skull.

Pfaff twisted and it hit—snapped—a collarbone instead.

In the same instant the chamber's door swung open. Two space-fleet guards gaped across the threshold.

Face twisted with pain, clutching at his shattered clavicle, Pfaff roared, "Get this stabat!"

DANE LUNGED for the doorway, swinging the yat-stick. It clipped the first guard alongside the jaw; dropped him in his tracks. Dane stiff-armed the second and sprinted off down the passageway.

But as he ran, alarm bells all about began to jangle. Ahead, a spaceman appeared as if from nowhere, paralyzer at the ready.

Dane veered into the first cross-passage; dropped down a pneumolift to the next level.

More green telonium walls. More bells and guards and paralyzers.

Lurching now, staggering, Dane stumbled onward. It was as if his body was acting independently, without his mind's volition, for intelligence told him flatly that there would be, could be, no escape. Not in a closed unit like a spaceship.

Yet here he was, still fleeing.

Why? Why?

Laughing, he downed another guard with the yat-stick; and even in his own ears his mirth rang a drunken note.

Another pneumolift. Another. And after that, a long, dim-lighted passage.

Dead end.

So this was where they'd trap him.

Only then, as he slumped to the floor, he stubbed his toe on a heavy screw-lock; saw at last the scarlet lidded hatch on which he squatted.

One more barrier to put behind him.

Wearily, he wrenched the screw locks open; pried up the spring catch; lifted the hatch-lid; peered down into the space beneath it.

An unpleasant, faintly musty odor. A wall-ladder leading down into pale grey emptiness.

Yat-stick still in hand, Dane lowered himself gingerly through the hatchway and let the heavy scarlet lid fall above him, wondering as he did so why it was painted so bright a red.

The spring catch clicked into place. No going back now.

Down the ladder, a rung at a time. Ten feet. Fifteen. Twenty.

Solid decking again. Solid…yet strangely slippery. And the unpleasant musty smell was stronger now, too.

Something brushed Dane's hand. Something gelatinous and clammy.

Instinctively, he jerked back.

His eyes were adjusting to the pale grey light now. He could see better.

He wished he couldn't.

Because the thing that had brushed his hand…the slimy, gelatinous thing that now was making the flesh crawl over every inch of his body…was a monstrous, many-eyed, pseudopodal horror he couldn't even classify.

But it could classify him, apparently; for already its amoeboid protrusions were eddying in close to his feet with tiny, obscene sucking noises.

Heart pounding, blood chilling, Dane gripped the yat-stick till his knuckles ached. At last—at last he knew why that hatch-lid overhead had been painted such a vivid scarlet.

It led into the spaceship's bem-tank!

## CHAPTER THREE

EVEN AS THE REALIZATION of where he stood at last bust upon Dane with full, nerve-shattering force, the creature confronting him moved forward, closing in about him in a half-moon arc that reached from wall to wall. How large it was, Dane could only guess, for it extended farther into the dimness than he could see, piling up in great, semi-transparent folds almost as high as his head in places, like some monstrous, shapeless jellyfish speckled with eyespots.

Now, while Dane watched, rigid, the creature put forth another pseudopod. Stickily, the protuberance crept along the metal tank wall, closer and closer.

A trickle of icy sweat rilled down Dane's spine. Numb, shallow-breathed, he drew back from the advancing tentacle of protoplasm.

In the same instant a chill, moist, odorous Something spewed onto the back of Dane's neck and shoulders; another pseudopod, moving in while the first held his attention.

With a wild yell, Dane lunged for the ladder; tried to claw his way up it.

But the pseudopod clung to him like some loathsome growth, part of him. Before he could tear free of it, the living wall about him swept in, a tide of protoplasm that in seconds mired him to the ankle...the knees...the waist...

Dane shrieked aloud. New strength flooded through him, born of sheer terror. Frantically, he lashed out with the yat-stick, flailing this way and that at the encroaching extraterrestrial horror that any moment now might swallow him completely.

But to no avail. Here and there where he struck, the monster's jelly-like tissue quivered a little under impact. That was all.

And still it oozed higher about him. It was to his chest now. His armpits.

Abruptly, Dane stopped flailing. What was the point of it, as things stood now? The best he could hope for was a quick and easy death.

Yet what a place to die, after all his efforts! Here, sealed away in a spaceship's bem-tank! Chances were no one would ever so much as find his body, nor any clue as to what had happened to him.

Which would be a joke of sorts on Pfaff...something to try to account for to Nelva Guthrie and his own superiors.

No doubt it would baffle the other man too, Dane decided—the Being-Without-A-Name, the mind-talker who'd spent so much time and effort trying to force subservience upon him.

Or did that strange hairless, hollow-eyed, fiend-faced man even exist? Thinking back over everything, Dane couldn't help but wonder. In retrospect, a nightmare quality clung to the whole incident, as if perhaps it were delusion, hallucination, rather than reality.

In any case, it didn't matter, because now, dying here, he'd never know.

And that was too bad, in a way, because there were so many things Dane knew in his heart he'd like to have uncovered. Things like the secret of his own identity, his past and future...the meaning of the shining shaft he'd seen and that he knew was somehow bound close to his own destiny...the business of the Kalquoi yat-stick, and how it came to be in the bleak asteroidal cave where the survey ship had found him.

The gelatinous mass had reached his neck now:   It wouldn't be much longer.

Dane laughed harshly.  "Come on, damn it!  Get it over with!"  He wrenched his right arm free; hurled the yat-stick out into the center of the viscid mass attacking him.

The ooze crept to his chin.  Time stood still, every second dragging out to an eternity.

Dane closed his eyes.

As if it were a signal, a rhythm seemed to start up in his brain:  *Dane...Dane...Dane...*

His own name, endlessly repeated.  The beginning of a death-throe madness, perhaps, Dane decided with a queer sense of abstraction.

Like magic, the pattern changed:   *John Dane...John Dane...John Dane...*

In spite of himself, Dane felt a quick-glowing spark of interest.  Almost without volition, he spoke aloud:  "Not John Dane.  Clark Dane."

The rhythm in his brain faltered; broke.  In its place came a vague uneasiness, a restless groping:  *Clark Dane—?  Clark Dane?  No, no.  John Dane.  JOHN Dane!*

"CLARK Dane," Dane reiterated firmly.

INSTANTLY, the previous uneasiness returned, but multiplied a hundred-fold.  Needles of pain shot through his brain.  The pale grey emptiness of his prison vanished in a blaze of purple light.  Even the gelatinous sea of protoplasm enveloping Dane seemed to transmit a sudden shiver.

Dane opened his eyes.

But the purple light was no pain-born illusion. Rather, it glinted even brighter now than before.

Its source was a crystal...a strange, radiant crystal that floated before Dane in mid-air.

Now, while he watched, the purple light changed to green; then red; then yellow.

The crystal, too, was changing. Before his eyes, it writhed and stretched until it was a glowing aquamarine ladder, modeled after the one down which Dane had come into the bem-tank.

A moment later it was a bright blue bottle; then a cerise cube; then once again a crystal, orange and golden.

And all the time, the turmoil in Dane's brain continued...a chaotic, inarticulate fumbling, based on some point of confusion between the two names, *John* and *Clark*.

But despite the pain, Dane hardly noticed the groping and the searching. He had mind only for the colored light and changing shape of the weird crystal that hovered before him.

For there was only one thing it could be: a Kalquoi, one of those dreaded alien invaders who'd long since usurped the outer planets, beyond the asteroid belt.

Now it was here, on this ship, headed straight for Mars!

And there was nothing he could do about it.

As if to emphasize the point, the amoeboid monster in whose grip he lay pushed a new pseudopod down upon Dane's head and face. Oozing, enveloping, smothering, it pressed into every pore and orifice.

Dane gasped for breath that would not come. Choking, jerking, convulsing, he struggled against he mucilaginous mass that held him.

It was like fighting quicksand. The creature would not let him go. Fire raced through Dane's lungs. Black fog rose, clouding his consciousness. He forgot who he was and where he was, and even the pulsing pain of the Kalquoi's sentient probings.

Slowly, then faster and faster: he began to fall...to fall...

Only then, of a sudden, his mouth and nose, his face, were clear again. Spasmodically, Dane sucked air into his lungs in great, anguished gasps.

When his knees gave way, he slumped to the slime-slick floor.

It dawned on him dimly, then, that the monster had left him...that he was free and safe once more.

Why?

Still not quite steady, he looked out across the bem-tank; saw the protoplasmic horror huddled in a quaking, quivering mass against the chamber's far wall. The Kalquoi hovered above it; and when the giant amoeba-thing made a tentative effort to ooze back in Dane's direction, the alien assailed it with sudden, darting light-beams that seared deep into the pseudopodal creature's tissue.

The demonstration was enough for Dane: the Kalquoi had saved him.

But again, why?

It was a question without an answer—or, at least, with no answer Dane himself could fathom. Besides, for now, it was enough that he remained alive. Puzzles could come later.

Meanwhile—

But before he could organize the thought, sound came into the tank's stillness: the creak of screw locks turning; the clink of a spring catch released.

For the barest instant the Kalquoi hovered as if listening. Then, like a candle snuffed out, it vanished.

Dane surged to his feet. Darting across the slippery decking, he found the yat-stick and, snatching it up, stuffed it out of sight beneath his tunic.

Simultaneously, a sudden draft told him the hatch was open. Light blazed—a brilliant beam that pinned Dane, half-blinded, to the tank's wall.

Yet in spite of his situation, he could not repress a momentary grin. It would be worth a good deal of discomfort just to watch Pfaff's reaction when he found victim alive and monster cowed!

Then a guard called down to Dane, ordering him up the ladder and out of the tank. Brief minutes later, two other spacemen escorted him to the threshold of a room ornate enough for Dane to assume that it must be the captain's office.

THE DOOR GUARD ordered a halt. Beyond him, Dane could glimpse Pfaff, standing inside the office. But the Security rep's whole manner proved a disappointment. Far from ranting, he wore an air of sullen, savage, inadequately repressed fury. The thick, bruised tips were drawn tight, the bullet head tilted forward a fraction as if to avoid someone's gaze.

Then the guard pushed Dane forward again, and he saw the reason for the Security man's manner.

For Nelva Guthrie and the spaceship's captain stood side by side across from Pfaff. The officer, bland-faced, stared toward the far corner of the ceiling, and Dane interpreted the way the man's mouth twisted to mean that this was a moment long anticipated and thoroughly savored.

But no trace of amusement showed in Nelva Guthrie's pale, lovely face. Eyes blazing, she lanced barbed words straight at Pfaff: "—and so, in spite of the protests of this ship's officers, you intentionally and maliciously violated my orders, Mr. Pfaff?"

Muttered incoherence.

"Answer me, Mr. Pfaff!"

"Not maliciously, I said."

"Oh, really, Mr. Pfaff?" Nelva Guthrie's grey eyes sparked. The ash blonde hair rippled as she tossed her head in a quick, impatient movement. "What would you call it, then, when you abuse a man to the point that he takes refuge in a bem-tank, after I've particularly emphasized its vital not to upset him?"

A mumble.

"Speak up, Mr. Pfaff!"

"All right, I will!" All at once the other seemed to have lost all control over his temper. The massive shoulders hunched forward; the lumpy face thrust out, bold and belligerent, in the manner of the Pfaff whom Dane remembered. "I wanted to know how come this chitza got stranded on that asteroid. I still do, and I'm going to find out, even with you here."

"Indeed?"

"You bet indeed! You think Security moves over for every little bobtailed slazot out of Records? I'm rep on this ship, and I'm labeling this whole business as Security jurisdiction! You don't like it, you can state your case to Thorburg Jessup!"

Color came to the girl's cheeks. Her voice, icy calm, dropped even lower than before. "How old do you think I am, Mr. Pfaff?"

"How old—?" The Security rep stared; stumbled. "How should I know? What's that got to do with this?"

"You'll see. Meanwhile, please make an estimate."

"Well...maybe twenty-five."

"You're quite close. I'm twenty-six."

"So ?"

"So how many twenty-six-year old women do you know who are supervisors of planetary record centers?"

Pfaff's mouth opened, then closed again with no word uttered.

Nelva Guthrie said, "Some men, Mr. Pfaff, might deduce from this that such a woman has certain—contacts."

The Security agent still held his silence.

"In my case," the girl went on, "the contacts are more than adequate." A slight tightening of the lips. "Mr. Jessup no doubt will tell you all about it when he calls you."

Pfaff's broad face went suddenly slack. The close-set eyes drew down to gimlets. "What do you mean, damn you?"

"I mean you've finally overreached yourself, Mr. Pfaff," Nelva Guthrie retorted icily. "Devotion to duty's one thing, self-glorification another. Not even Security will back a man who's so eager for advancement as to endanger a vital project in the remote hope he can bully his way through to personal credit."

"But—Jessup—"

"Why would he call you, you mean?" Nelva Guthrie looked the image of wide-eyed innocence. "Why, to relieve you, of course, Mr. Pfaff. Orders are already cleared for your suspension as Security rep for an indefinite period. You unload as soon as the ship ramps down on Mars."

Finality on a level that forbade dispute or question was in the girl's voice and manner. She turned from Pfaff; faced Dane for the first time.

It was a strange moment for him. For as he looked into her eyes, in that first fraction of a second, he saw things paradoxical, things wholly unexpected…discernment, warmth, concern, a tender questioning.

It rocked Dane back, almost unbelieving.

Then the moment faded, as if a blind had snapped shut somewhere behind the clear grey eyes. Smiling, yet brisk and businesslike, Nelva crossed to him and extended a slim, firm hand. "Mr. Dane, I can't tell you how happy I am to see you.

The Mars Record Center definitely considers itself fortunate to have the opportunity to study your case at first hand."

Wryly, Dane matched her smile. "I'm hardly uninterested myself."

"The sooner we get to it, the better, then. My carrier's waiting."

Nelva's smile was ever so bright. Yet looking from her to the bland-faced spaceship captain and sullen-eyed, hate-glowering Pfaff, Dane felt a sudden, swift wave of uneasiness.

This business—somehow, it was all too neatly organized, too smooth.

But there was nothing he could do about it. Not now; not till he knew more.

"All right with me," he shrugged. "Let's go."

Did the blind behind Nelva's eyes flicker for the barest instant? He wondered.

"Good!" Impulsively, it seemed, she caught his hand. "This way—"

Wordless, taut-nerved, looking neither to right nor left, Dane walked with her from the room.

## CHAPTER FOUR

IT WAS QUIET, here in Nelva Guthrie's office in the Record Center. She said, "It takes a few minutes for the cell-sheets to come through, Mr. Dane, and I know you must be tired. Why don't you lie down on the couch while we're waiting?"

"Thanks. I will." Gratefully, Dane stretched out; drank in the cool greens and soft blues of the decor. The climatizer's rhythmic whisper lulled him.

Yet restful though it all was, complete relaxation somehow would not come. In spite of all his efforts, Dane found himself heir to twitching muscles, sudden tensing. Half a dozen times, he caught himself watching Nelva sidewise as she checked through a pile of papers, as if he were afraid to leave her unobserved.

Why? Because he felt drawn to her as a woman? Because he feared that she might slip away?

Or, because the contrast between the mask of distance she now wore, as compared to the things he'd seen when their eyes first met, was so marked as to make him permanently wary, unwilling to trust her?

The thought set irritation pricking at him. Abruptly, he sat up. "It's no use."

"To try to rest, you mean, when you don't know who you are or where you come from?"

"That's right." Dane spread his hands in a helpless gesture. "Why should I be the first man in more than a hundred years to have this happen to him? You said yourself amnesia's been wiped out."

"True enough," the woman nodded, ash-blonde hair shimmering. "In your case, however, some rather unusual factors complicate the picture."

Dane frowned. "What kind of factors?"

For a long moment Nelva studied him, as if debating. Then, at last, she said, "I guess there's no real harm in telling you. The reason we know you're a victim of amnesia is because the survey ship's psychman ran a narcoanalysis on you. And what you thought was a perception test, downstairs here, was really a hypnoanalysis to check the psychman's findings."

"So?"

"The results were most interesting. For one thing, you didn't respond to treatment. Amnesia's an adaptive reaction to inner conflict, a sort of hysterical inhibition. When the inhibition's released by the Egrisanto technique, under deep analysis, ordinarily the block to memory goes with it, and recall returns." Nelva ran a slim forefinger along the edge of her papers; eyed Dane. "Do you follow me?"

Dane nodded slowly. "I think so."

"Then you'll understand how it startled me when I found no trace of any real inhibition, no sensitive areas you were trying to protect." Nelva spread her hands. "As a matter of fact you reacted freely on every subject covered by the standard tests. And you showed a rather remarkable fund of information on virtually every topic."

Dane groped. "Then what—?"

"Don't you see? You're holding back nothing...yet there's not even the slightest hint as to when that knowledge came from! It's almost as if you were a robot, with built-in reaction patterns and knowledge tapes instead of a human brain."

A chill ran through Dane. He sat very still.

What was it the fiend-faced man, the Being-Without-A-Name, had said to him in those first delirious moments of his awareness that now seemed so long ago—? "Bow down to your creator?"

Involuntarily, Dane shuddered.

Nelva said, "You're thinking about your dream, aren't you? About how the man said he'd created you?" Her voice was warm with sympathy.

Dane looked up sharply. "How did you know—?"

"Simple logic. The analysis gave me all the things in your mind—about the man with the hairless skull who was your master, and the silver needle, and the Kalquoi. When I mentioned robots, it was almost certain to make you think about—the man."

"Oh."

"You don't need to worry, either. You're not a robot. Robots don't have feelings. Besides, the celloscope would have shown it if you were. As for the rest—the shaft—the Kalquoi—I imagine they're some sort of delusion. Tied in with your amnesia, perhaps—specialized situations the standard tests weren't geared to touch."

"I see." Dane studied his knuckles.

Yet what did he see? What, really? He wondered.

Certainly not that the fiend-faced man and the silver needle and the Kalquoi were delusions!

For as Nelva talked, her words had come faster and faster. A new note had crept into her voice—a note of tension. And now, as he watched her obliquely, he became acutely aware that her fingers were all at once ever so restless. Her lips showed a minute tendency to tremble, also, and the grey eyes stayed clear of him, as if the things she said were creating some undercurrent of conflict in her that she feared to let him see.

DANE'S JAW tightened. Breathing carefully, evenly, he thought back once again to the way the girl had first looked at him—and then, how the blinds had come down, shutting him out.

How could he trust this woman, while that hidden barrier in her eyes still stood between them? How dared he throw aside all suspicion, all caution, so long as she held back secrets?

No; at root the dilemma still was his, and always would be. Not even Nelva Guthrie could share it with him. He had no choice but to go his own road, fight through to his private destiny.

And what better time to start than now?

Tight-lipped, he said, "All this is fine. But it looks to me like it's going in a circle."

Nelva's hands moved nervously. Her eyes opened a trifle wider than seemed normal. "A circle—?"

"You claim I've got amnesia, don't you? Only then you tell me I don't react right for it." Dane laughed, harsh and curt. "To me, that says we're getting nowhere."

A knock broke off the conversation. Quickly, as if relieved at the interruption, Nelva crossed the room and opened the door.

A uniformed tech held out a plastic cylinder. "Here's that cellsheet, Miss Guthrie."

"Good!" There was an air of relief in the way Nelva said it. She turned to Dane; gestured triumphantly with the cylinder. "This is the answer to your problems, Clark! Your cellemental analysis sheet! Come on!"

Shrugging, Dane fell in beside her. He wondered wryly how he had so suddenly been promoted to first-name status.

Nelva was still talking: "A cellsheet's proof positive of identity, Clark. By Federation law, one's made for every human at birth among the inner planets. All records on that person then are filed under the cell-sheet's pattern. So you won't be a lost soul much longer. Two minutes after we put this cylinder into the interplanetary index system, we'll know everything there is to know about you…"

They were in another room now—a long, narrow room through which busy techs hurried. The walls on either side were banked solid, floor to ceiling, with varicolored index flashers. A black, box-like unit, shoulder-high, occupied the center of the floor. Beyond it, at the room's far end, double doors like those through which Dane and Nelva had just entered provided a second exit.

"This way," Nelva commanded briskly. Leading Dane to the boxlike unit, she flipped open one of a row of hinged cases lining each edge, fitted Dane's cell-sheet onto a spool, closed the lid once more, and pressed a button.

She kept up a running fire of small-talk as she worked. It came out just a trifle too animated. Dane decided her primary purpose was to forestall embarrassing questions rather than to convey data.

Now she pointed to a slot below the cylinder-spool. "This is the place, Clark. And in just two minutes!"

In spite of himself, Dane didn't tear his eyes from the slot.

Seconds, ticking by…dragging out to what seemed eons…

Then a bell rang, a single sharp, imperative note. A card spilled from the slot.

It seemed to Dane for an instant as if Nelva had stiffened. A nearby tech looked up sharply.

But Nelva's hand was darting out. Deftly, she caught the card before it reached the tray and, turning, studied it. Whether by accident or design, her body shielded the record so Dane couldn't see it. When he would have stepped round her, she flipped the card over and stood scrutinizing the punch-marks and code-symbols on the reverse side.

Dane held his voice level. "Well? What does it say?"

"Say—? Oh, it—it tells the file we have to send to for your records."

But Nelva's voice shook. Her face had paled. Tight-lipped, Dane body-blocked her against the machine and snatched the card from her; turned it over.

The legend's top line was printed in red letters a good inch tall:

## NO RECORD

And then, a little bit smaller, beneath it:

## HOLD SUBJECT IN TOP SECURITY ISOLATION PENDING INTENSIVE INVESTIGATION AND APPROPRIATE TESTS FOR PSYCHOPATHY, CRIMIN-ALITY, AND FOR POSSIBLE KALQUOI CONNECTIONS.

# CHAPTER FIVE

WORDS ON A CARD. That was all they were. But they spelled an end to hope.

Numbly, Dane looked at Nelva.

White to the lips, she dodged his gaze.

But beyond her, over by the door through which they'd entered, a man who wore a guard's uniform had suddenly appeared and now stood to one side, scanning the index-chamber.

While Dane watched, two more guards joined the first.

Dane crowded close to Nelva. His words came out a raw whisper: "Those guards—are they after me?"

She didn't answer.

Dane's belly knotted. His hands shook.

But he couldn't afford the luxury of cracking. Not now, of all times.

No. The only course open now was to follow desperation's dictates.

Psychopath? Criminal? Kalquoi agent?

If those were his labels, he might as well live up to them!

Grimly, he let his hand brush the heavy yat-stick still concealed beneath his tunic; forced his face into the caricature of a grin as he gazed at Nelva.

The girl seemed scarcely to be breathing.

Dane said softly, "We're getting out of this place. You and me, together. We're going to walk through the entry door at the far end of this room. Understand?"

Nelva's eyes distended, wide with sudden panic. Her mouth started to open.

Dane caught her wrist in a savage grip; twisted so sharply she came forward on tiptoe, face drawn with pain. "Scream and I'll break your arm!"

Only the faintest flicker of Nelva's lids indicated that she'd heard him. But she turned as he did under the pressure on her wrist and moved with him in the direction of the doorway.

Behind them, a loud voice cried, "Hey, there!"

Dane flung a quick glance back; glimpsed the guards starting towards him.

With a curse, he shoved Nelva forward, ahead of him, in a frantic dash for the door.

They made it in a rush. Feeling the panel shut in the faces of his pursuers, Dane wheeled right down the corridor.

But even as he turned, he came face to face with yet another guard, charging up the hall straight at him.

Savagely, Dane flung Nelva aside. Clawing out the yat-stick, he smashed its heavy head to the pit of the man's stomach.

The guard bent double. Bowling him out of the way, Dane pivoted, braced for attack or flight alike.

Yet to what end? In his heart, he knew it would be the same here as on the spaceship. Sooner or later, his adversaries would hunt him down; trap him...

Then, off to his left, a voice cried, "Clark! This way!"

Nelva's voice.

Dane whirled; glimpsed the girl beckoning frantically from an alcove. Sprinting to her, he crowded past a door that she held open, and into a cramped, shadowy chamber beyond.

"Now, here..." Nelva's hand caught his, leading him onward.

Another door. Another. A room piled high with stored furniture and equipment.

Nelva said, "You can hide here for a little while. After that…" Her voice trailed off. She was breathing hard.

Dane said, "I'm tired of hiding. It gets me nowhere."

The girl's grey eyes widened. "But—what—?"

"Which way to your analytical computer?"

"Analytical computer—?" Nelva looked bewildered. "What computer? What are you talking about?"

"You know what I mean!" Dane bared his teeth. "Every planetary record center's built around one. It's the gadget that organizes your information, sorts out your data, makes your decisions when you've got too many complicating factors for a human mind to handle." He laughed harshly. "That's me, right now. I'm up against too many complicating factors. So I'm going to ask your computer for some answers."

NELVA STARED at him incredulously. "Are you mad, Clark? At best, we've a few minutes' freedom for you. No more. Any moment, Security may send someone in here—"

"That's why I won't wait for them!" Dane came back fiercely. "Sure, you saved my neck, dragging me in here. I'm grateful for it. But not so grateful I'm willing to stand waiting till someone hunts me down." He hammered a clenched fist into his palm. "No, damn it! I'll do some of the hunting this time. And that starts with some questions for your computer!"

"But what—?"

"What questions?" Dane laughed again. "Can't you guess? I want to know that man who claimed I was his slave. About the silver needle. The Kalquoi. Who I am; why I can't remember anything; how it is I've no record in your files. Maybe even about you and what you're up to. Things like that, a lot of them."

New lines etched Nelva's lovely face. "Clark, you can't!"

"Can't I?" Dane paced the floor. "Take me there and we'll see whether I can or not!"

"No, no! You don't understand." Nelva's hands moved in a gesture of frustration. "It's just, not that easy to use an analytical computer."

Dane stopped his pacing. He frowned. "How's that?"

"For one thing, the machine's self-limiting. It covers only certain areas of information, likely to be needed here on Mars. But your questions aren't localized."

"Give me an example."

"The Kalquoi. They're a menace to all the inner planets, not just Mars. So when you ask about them, the only answer our machine will give you is a referral to the big System Computer on Luna."

"Go on."

"Even setting up a question properly can take weeks. You have to be sure it's framed within the machine's limitations. Take this man you talk about. I wouldn't begin to know how to key a query on him, with nothing to start from but your verbal description of an emotionalized visual image."

"I see."

"It's the same with the silver needle. How do you classify it—as art, armament, or industrial equipment?"

Dane nodded slowly. "You make a good case, Nelva." And then: "But I'll still have a try at it. Let's go."

The girl stared at him, and before his eyes the shreds of her earlier composure vanished. "Clark, I won't let you do it!"

Wordless, Dane reached for her arm.

She didn't even try to jerk back. Her words came in a rush: "Clark, you don't understand! Security keeps guards on all computers—a special unit of Thorburg Jessup's private zombies. They'd capture you or kill you before you even got close to the question boards—"

"That would make a difference to you?"

"Can I say it any plainer?" The girl's lips trembled. She caught Dane's hand between hers. "I won't let them get you, Clark! I won't! That's why I'm telling you these things; why I've tried to help you. We'll find some place to hide you, somehow, where even Security can't find you—"

"Sorry, Nelva." Dane shook his head. "I'm not fool enough to think I can hide from Security, even if I wanted to. And as for what you say about the computer—well, this is my day to see things for myself."

Nelva drew back. Her nostrils were flaring, yet she seemed closer to tears than anger. "You don't trust me!"

"That's right. I don't." Dane made it flat and brutal.

"But I—I've helped you—"

"Right again. But the way things stack up, I'm not sure why. So till I know for sure, I'll play it my way." Dane bit down hard, fighting down all impulses to warmth and tenderness. "We'll have a look at that computer now."

"Clark, wait—!"

"Well?"

"You won't have to go to the computer. I'll tell you—"

Nelva broke off raggedly. She was breathing too fast, and her eyes held a strange, wild look.

Dane stared. "You'll tell me what?"

"About the silver shaft, the needle. That's the only one of your questions I know anything about." The girl came up against him; clung to him, her face an anguished mask. "I wasn't lying about the computer, either, Clark. It is guarded by those awful creatures Jessup's biochemists have bred in the Mercury labs. You wouldn't stand a chance against them. That's why I couldn't let you go there. They're completely ruthless—all duty conditioning, not a trace of human feeling in any of them—"

"Forget about that!" Dane gripped her arms. "Tell me about the shaft. That's what I want to know!"

"It's—it's on Callisto—"

"Callisto—?" Dane stared. "That's Kalquoi territory, isn't it?"

"Yes, of course. They occupied it when they took over the outer planets thirty years ago."

"Then the shaft—"

"—is a relic of the days just before the occupation," Nelva finished for Dane. "It was a weapon, Clark—a weapon set up at Sandoz, the chief human city on Callisto. The Sandoz Shaft, they called it. Only then it didn't work, so people ended up saying it was the Sandoz Tombstone. It's mentioned in all the Kalquoi Invasion knowledge tapes. That's how I know about it."

PRICKLES OF EXCITEMENT ran up and down Dane's spine. For the first time he began to feel as if he were making progress, coming to grips with the mysteries which seemed ever to surround him.

"Do you know any more about the thing?" he demanded of Nelva. "How was it supposed to work? What went wrong?"

The girl's smooth brow furrowed in concentration. "As I recall, the shaft was nothing but a gigantic Udellian transmitter."

"A Udellian transmitter—?"

"Yes. Back when the Kalquoi first came to our system, someone discovered that high-frequency Udellian waves kept them from changing shape or swallowing up things. And if the amplification was strong enough, the waves would even shatter the crystals, the Kalquoi bodies. That was the whole idea behind the shaft: to destroy the Kalquoi if they tried to attack Sandoz."

"And what happened?"

Nelva shrugged slim shoulders. "I'm not enough of a tech in that field to tell you, really. But as I understand it, it turned out that the shaft was one of those things that works fine when you hold the size down to a laboratory model."

"But when they increased the size it wouldn't work?"

"That's right," Nelva nodded. "It seems that when the transmitter got beyond a certain size, the amount of power it took climbed way out of proportion—so much so the available broadcast relay equipment couldn't even activate the shaft, let alone make it effective against the Kalquoi."

"So?"

"So the Kalquoi came, and Sandoz—all Callisto—was abandoned." Nelva lifted her hands in a small, sad gesture. "That's all I know, Clark. Every bit."

Dane nodded slowly.

Nelva said, "I'm afraid that's the way it may turn out with all your questions. There won't be any answers—not real answers; not the kind that can help you. That's why I'm so anxious to see to it Security doesn't find you."

Dane pondered her words for a long, dragging moment. Finally he asked, "Where's that carrier you picked me up in?"

The girl shot him a quick glance. "The carrier—?" And then: "Why, on the roof here, I guess. But of course it's just short-range—"

"Do you think we could get to it?"

"Perhaps." Nelva studied him thoughtfully. "Surely you're not really thinking of trying to get away from Security in a carrier, are you?"

Dane grinned, a trifle thinly. "You never can quite tell about me, can you?" He let the grin develop into a chuckle. "How do we get up there, anyhow?"

"There's a pneumolift. Right through this door…" But though Nelva led the way, a shadow lay across her face that might have been irritation, or bafflement, or both.

It was strangely quiet in the building, it seemed to Dane. Especially considering there was a full-scale Security search for him in progress.

He tried not to think about it.

He was tense enough as it was, without letting his imagination run riot.

Obliquely, he stole a glance at Nelva Guthrie, beside him in the lift.

The shadow across her face had vanished. Now the girl seemed almost placid. It was as if, in her eyes, everything was going precisely according to plan.

DANE SMILED to himself a little at the thought…wondered how long she'd be able to hold to her complacency.

The pneumolift eased to a halt. Warily, Dane followed Nelva out…moved after her through the shadows to the carrier station.

Still no guards, no interruption.

A carrier, poised in its launching-rack, sleek-lined and graceful.

"There it is," Nelva whispered, gesturing. "Just be careful. It can't carry you much beyond the gravitational pull. You may end up playing tag with Phobos and Deimos!"

Dane noted that she stood well back, deep in the cover of the platform-beams.

Brooding, again he studied the carrier, so notably unguarded.

The silence echoed so loud it was making the skin along the back of his neck prickle.

Quite deliberately, then, he crossed to the cargo-ramp, making it a point to follow the shadows, close in to the platform-beams.

A stack of loading-cases stood beside the ramp. Pausing briefly, Dane glanced back to where Nelva still stood craning to watch him.

Then, with no warning, he whirled and threw his whole weight against the high-stacked cases.

For a moment they tottered on the ramp's edge. Then, with a crash like cataclysm incarnate, they tumbled down in an avalanche of ringing metal.

But even as they fell, Dane leaped back into the shadows once again. In a rush, he spanned the distance between him and Nelva.

She stared at him wide-eyed, mouth agape.

But only for a moment. For then, as water spews from a geyser, the carrier erupted guards—three of them.

From the level below, too, came the sound of running feet, converging on the cargo ramp.

Beside Dane, Nelva whispered, "What is it? What's happening?"

"A trap." Dane laughed harshly. "But of course you wouldn't know anything about that."

The girl's nostrils flared. "Are you trying to say something?"

For a moment Dane leaned forward, not answering.

Then, as the last of the guards disappeared down the cargo ramp, he spun about, swept the girl up bodily over his shoulder, and headed for the carrier at a dead run.

He was already on the loading ladder before the first shout of discovery arose behind him.

Inside, now. The hatch slammed shut. The launching lever pulled.

A sudden, swift sense of acceleration. Then the easing off as equalizer pressure rose to match it. In the viewer, Mars fell away beneath them.

Dane glanced at Nelva Guthrie.

She stood beside him, the lovely oval of her face a study in pallor. Her fingers trembled as she smoothed the ash-blonde hair, and fear flickered in the grey eyes.

"Clark, where are we going?" Her voice came out a ragged whisper. "Don't you realize they're sure to catch us?"

"Are they?" Dane chuckled grimly.

"Of course. They'll have every landing-platform covered."

Dane laughed again. It was incredible, how well he suddenly felt, all things considered. "Not ours they won't cover!" And then: "Because damn it, we're going straight to Callisto!"

## CHAPTER SIX

DANE STRETCHED the little carrier's resources to the limit, pushing it as far out from Mars as he could coax it.

Then, at last, when the craft was well established in a satellite orbit, between Phobos and Deimos and beyond all peril from the mother planet's gravitational pull, he cut the power, turned to the emergency distress-call communicator unit, and switched it on.

He knew Nelva's eyes were on him, even before he swung round to face her once again. It pleased him. How baffled she looked. But her lips stayed set in a thin, straight line—a memento of some of the things he'd said after the takeoff— so he knew she wouldn't speak till he did.

"All right," he grinned, "what do you give me for our chances now, my dear Miss Mars Record Center Supervisor Guthrie?"

The line of her mouth drew even tighter. So, after a moment, he let drive with another needle: "Or maybe, as an expert on problems and solutions, you don't want to give a dangerous Kalquoi agent like me the benefit of your professional opinion?"

That did it. Dane could see the girl's knuckles whiten. Her eyes flashed, more ice-blue now than grey.

"You're a fool, Clark Dane!" she burst out furiously. "Once that signal's picked up, Security's sure to have patrol ships here within an hour!"

"Maybe." Dane permitted himself the luxury of grim humor.

"No maybe! You know it's true!"

"Or, maybe not," Dane went on, with no heed to Nelva's interruption. "It might even be Security won't pay the first bit of attention to it." He shot a sidelong glance at the girl. "Would you like to ask me why?"

A moment of obvious, barely-repressed fury. Then: "Why?"

"Because not even a Kalquoi agent would be fool enough to try to get clear of Mars in a four-place carrier." Dane leaned back; stretched. "No; Security's not going to be looking up here for us. Not when they've got all those landing-platforms down below to cover."

It did him good to see the way Nelva's jaw slackened.

"Of course," he observed wryly, "that opens up another question, too, doesn't it?"

"Another question—?"

"Yes, you know: the question about how you and I are going to get to Callisto."

The last of the anger-lines vanished from Nelva's lovely face. Her lips parted, breathless with interest. "Tell me, Clark! Have you really devised a way to do it?"

"I think so." Dane paused, letting the moment's tension build up. And then: "Only of course that's no sign I'll tell you about it and give you a chance to sour it."

As knife-twisting, it came off very satisfactorily. Nelva's face went white as if he'd slapped it. Her eyes turned blank, hurt-emptied.

Inside, Dane cringed a little. Of a sudden he felt cheap, ashamed he'd resorted to such pettiness even in anger. Miserably, he turned to the viewer and rotated its field, searching the void about him.

But before he could so much as complete the circuit, the proximity magnetron's gong rolled brassily. Whipping round the viewer's field in the indicated direction, Dane discovered the cylindrical bulk of a cargo ship wheeling towards the carrier. While he watched, the pickup bay's gate slid back. Receiver racks swung out and clamped onto the smaller craft, then retracted once more, lifting the carrier into the yawning bay as the gate slid closed.

Dane ran his tongue along lips gone suddenly dry.

But now it was too late to turn back. Pushing up from his seat, he stepped quickly across to Nelva.

Something in his gaze must have warned her. Eyes wide with panic, she tried to jump up and scramble clear.

Timing his blow with cool deliberation, Dane drove a hard right to the point of her jaw.

The girl's head snapped back. She crumpled with an unhinged limpness that almost made Dane ill.

But com-box blared in the same instant: "Carrier! What's your trouble? Can you open your hatches or shall we cut our way in?"

It broke Dane's spell. Snapping on the carrier's box, he bent close: "I've got a girl aboard here. She's hurt pretty bad. You'd better come prepared to take her off. As to the how and why of it all—well, probably the best thing would be to have your captain come in first and look it over."

"The captain—!" The spaceship's amplifier squawked protestingly. "Listen, mister—"

"To hell with that! You listen!" Dane tried to match the harsh belligerence of the performance Pfaff, the Security rep, had given aboard the survey ship. "I've got the kind of trouble here it's going to take top rank to handle, and I'm not going to waste time talking about it, either. Just see that your captain's the first man to come aboard this carrier. If he's not, I won't take responsibility for anything that happens— and plenty will, believe me!"

DANE SNAPPED off the carrier's com-box as he finished. Wryly, he wondered what the spaceship's officers would conjure up as being the situation aboard the carrier. Certainly he'd given them no grounds for peace of mind!

But now it was time for him to prepare to receive the captain. Taking the yat-stick from beneath his tunic, he wrapped it hastily in loose plastic strips torn from the carrier's sleeper sheaths till it made a bundle about the same size and shape as his own head.

Then a knocking at the hatch told him his visitor had arrived. Gripping the bundle containing the yat-stick firmly beneath his arm, Dane levered open the hatch-cover and looked out gravely at the little knot of men who stood waiting on the spaceship's transfer platform. "Which one of you's the captain?"

A tall, thin, horse-faced officer with coarse grey hair, protruding eyes and an uncertain manner gestured diffidently. "Well, I am. Einar Helstrom. Captain Helstrom, that is…"

"Good." Dane tried to look even more solemn than before. "Captain, this is the kind of emergency that's for your eyes alone. I wouldn't want to expose anyone else to it till you've passed judgment."

He stepped aside as he spoke. After a moment's uncertainty and nervous shifting from foot to foot, Captain Helstrom in his turn swung aboard and uneasily stepped down into the carrier's passenger compartment.

As he did so, Nelva Guthrie moaned.

The captain tripped over his own feet getting to one side. Eyes seeming to protrude even more than usual, he peered down at the prostrate girl, then turned to Dane. "What— what is it? What's the matter?"

Dane shrugged. "A little fainting spell. She'll be all right in a few minutes But this"—a brief pause while he held out the package containing the yat-stick—"is something else again."

Captain Helstrom eyed the package fearfully. "What's in it?"

Dane returned the bundle to its place tight-clamped beneath his arm before answering. Then, quite deliberately and with an almost academic manner, he asked, "Captain, do you know what a proton grenade is?"

"A proton grenade—!" The captain's jaw dropped, lengthening his face so that he looked more like a horse than ever. "Not those things they tried out against the Kalquoi once, you don't mean? Not the ones that could tear a whole ship apart from just a little hand bomb?"

He backed away with little teetering steps as he spoke, halting only when he bumped against the wall of the carrier's cabin.

"That's right," Dane nodded. "Have you ever seen one?" And then, shoving forward the yat-stick package and stripping away the outer layer of plastic till the T's crossbar was revealed: "See, here's the trigger-release mechanism—"

"Please, mister!" Helstrom croaked, bony hands spread as he tried to push Dane back. "Please, I don't want to see nothing. Nothing!"

"Well, if you don't want to..." Scowling irritably, as if disappointed, Dane wadded the plastic back over the end of the yat-stick. "You know who I am, captain?"

"N-no."

"Clark Dane, that's what they call me. Security's after me."

The captain's eyes bugged even further, and his Adam's apple moved up and down. He didn't speak.

Dane went on: "They thought they had me, down on Mars. I got away, though. Dug this"—he patted his bundle grimly—"out of a Security arsenal to bring with me."

The horse-face worked. The coarse grey hair appeared close to standing on end.

Dane scowled more ferociously than ever—as much to keep from laughing himself as to impress the captain. There was something so intrinsically absurd about the whole situation that he knew that one misstep would carry him over into gails of wild, hysterical mirth.

"Captain," he clipped tightly, "how'd you like to have me blow up this ship?"

Whatever it was the captain answered, Dane couldn't understand it. He pressed on: "There's just one way to save yourself, captain. That's to take me where I want to go. Because even if you hit me from behind—stun me, kill me—this grenade will still go off. The trigger's already free. This wrapping's the only thing that's holding it."

The captain gulped—a hollow, dyspeptic sound. "Wh-where do you want to go?" he asked finally.

Dane grinned. "Callisto."

"Callisto!" The grey hair was certainly sticking straight out now. "Mister, why don't you talk about Alpha Centauri or the Coalsack? They'd be every bit as easy!"

"Oh?"

"Security's got the Belt guarded like a vault. They'd brain-drain us before we were half-way through."

"You could set the guides for Callisto before we hit the Belt, couldn't you?"

"A computer-guide ramping on a satellite clear on the other side of the Asteroid Belt, with Jupiter's gravity pull to figure for?" Captain Helstrom shuddered. "Mister, you don't know what you're asking me for. Better to blow up your bomb now and be done with it!"

"Fair enough, if that's the way you feel about it," Dane agreed. He started to unwrap the yat-stick.

As if on springs, Helstrom sprang at him. "No, no, mister! I didn't mean it! We'll go; we'll go!"

Bleakly, Dane nodded. "I thought you might see it that way. So let's get started. And just for safety's sake, to make sure you don't change your mind—I'll stay right in your astrogation chamber with you!"

## CHAPTER SEVEN

AHEAD, THE BELT began to take form on the visiscreen—a patternless, ever-shifting array of hundreds of asteroids of every size and shape, all gleaming bright against the black-velvet backdrop of the void as they wheeled slowly through their far-flung orbits.

The vastness of it brought a sense of awe to Clark Dane.

Awe mixed with despondency and depression.

What chance did one man stand, trying to pick up the thin, tenuous thread of his destiny in this trackless chasm that was outer space? How could he hope to find identity, in a gulf so boundless that whole worlds were forever lost?

He'd been mad even to think—to dream—of choosing such a course.

Yet had he really chosen it? Was it truly his own will that had brought him to this moment?

Bleakly, he wondered; and as he did so, the old, infuriating sense of being a pawn in all he did...driven by another, larger will...swept over him once more.

Was he really a slave, thrall to the hairless man, the Being-Without-A-Name? Was it some darkly subtle conditioning, rather than his own impulses, that drove him?

Again...always; forever... Dane wondered...

But now, abruptly, the ship's com-box came to life to interrupt him: "Cargo Vessel 214XB7! Cargo Vessel 214XB7!"

It brought Dane back to the here-and-now—the cramped, instrument-banked, astrogation chamber of the spaceship. Gripping the yat-stick package tighter than ever, he tore his eyes from the wonders spread on the visiscreen and once again looked on horse faced Captain Helstrom and pale, silent, tight-lipped Nelva Guthrie.

The com-box blared again: "Cargo Vessel 214XB7! Acknowledge, Cargo Vessel 214XB7!"

"That's us," the grey-haired captain grunted. He started to reach for the switch to the ship's own communicator unit.

Dane caught his arm. "No."

"What—?" The captain's protruding eyes fixed on Dane uneasily. "You can't just ignore that call, mister. That's a Security blockade station. Stall 'em and they'll throw their brain-drain on you!"

Dane laughed harshly. "They'll do it anyhow, won't they, when they find we're heading through the Belt?"

The captain's Adam's apple bobbed. His narrow horse-face drew longer than ever. "Well…yes, I guess so."

"Get ready for it, then. Set your guides."

"On Callisto…?"

"On Callisto."

A shudder ran through the captain. "You ever been brain-drained, mister?"

"No."

"Well, I have, and it ain't fun. You're out of control. Completely."

A tiny chill touched the nape of Dane's neck. Out of the corner of his eye he could see Nelva watching him—the first hint she'd given that she knew he existed since they'd reached the astrogation chamber.

Once more, the com-box: "What the devil's the matter with you, 214? This is Security talking! We want an acknowledgment right now! You're already into blockade area. Wheel around fast, back away from the Belt, or we'll slap a drain on you!"

Another voice—this one from the amplifier of the ship's own communications network: "Captain Helstrom! Security's trying to get you! They say you're headed into the Belt! Is something wrong? Your door's locked. We can't get in to you…"

Dane ran his tongue along his lips. He could feel his companions' eyes upon him. The tension in the astrogation chamber was soaring higher every second.

"Cargo Vessel 214XB7, this is a last warning! Acknowledge this call and turn back at once! Failure to comply within thirty seconds will result in disabling dynamoencephalolytic action! Repeat, failure to comply within thirty seconds will result in disabling dynamoencephalolytic action…"

The captain and Nelva Guthrie, staring…gleaming pinpoints on a darkened visiscreen…a silver shaft and a hairless ghoul who laughed and laughed…

Dane sucked in air. "Are your guides set, Captain?"

"Computer guides set." Resignation and despair mixed in the greying officer's voice.

"For Callisto?"

"For Callisto."

Seconds, ticking by. Dane counted them as they passed.

Fifteen to go. Ten. Five. Four. Three. Two. One…

Nothing happened. Frowning, Dane started to turn to Helstrom.

IT HIT HIM, then—a sudden blazing bolt of power that surged and seethed through his brain. Dimly, as from afar, he was aware that the yat-stick package had slipped from his grasp and fallen to the floor, the truth as to its contents revealed as the plastic covering fell away. For his own part, a strange paralysis seemed to grip him. He stood upright, erect as before; yet it was beyond his power to move a single muscle. Sight and hearing—he still had them, but with vastly limited acuity. And while his brain still functioned, it seemed to work slowly, painfully, as if laboring under almost more of a burden than it could bear.

The captain and Nelva remained within the far periphery of his vision. Like him, both stayed motionless, frozen in the stance in which the brain-drain had trapped them.

Now Dane focused on the visiscreen. Moment by moment, it gave him the record of the course the robot-directed spaceship followed. Asteroids loomed, big and small; then disappeared once more.

How long that phase went on, Dane never knew. His sense of time was far too warped to allow for even a reasonably intelligent estimate.

But finally, the last of the asteroids fell away. Slowly, almost imperceptibly at first, the great globe of giant Jupiter moved in from the lower left corner of the screen.

Numbly, Dane watched and wondered. What, if anything, would he find at Sandoz? Or would the city even be there ? No one could say for sure, for no human had set foot on Callisto in the thirty years since it had been abandoned to the Kalquoi.

Only then, before he could even glimpse any of the satellites that swept around Jupiter, a new object flashed onto the visiscreen.

It was close, this one—so close that if he'd had the power, Dane would have covered his eyes out of sheer panic. Ball-round, the thing at first looked for all the world like a wandering asteroid or, perhaps, a giant meteor.

Yet there was a strange sheen about it; a too-perfect symmetry.

For a long moment, it hovered so close that it occupied almost half of the visiscreen. Then, suddenly, a light blazed from a point close to its perimeter: a tight cone of blinding radiance that turned the whole viewing plate white.

The next instant, the visiscreen went dead.

The lights died, too—all save the self-contained, dimly-luminous emergency radiation lamps. The rhythmic throbbing of the ventilating system halted also. So did the force drive's heavier beat. A sudden, incredible feeling of lightness came over Dane. Then his angle of view changed, and he realized that—unaware—he'd drifted clear of the floor; was now floating in midair. So the artificial gravity was off too.

A numb horror crept through him in the same instant. In his mind he cursed himself for a blind, imperceptive fool.

The thing he'd seen on the now blank screen was no asteroid or meteor, but a globe-ship, a Kalquoi globe-ship!

And the light was some sort of energy-diverting ray that had the power to incapacitate spaceship equipment.

So this was the end of his mad venture: not at Sandoz, not on Callisto, but here, aboard this crippled craft, destined perhaps to drift forever in blackness on the void-tides between the Asteroid Belt and the Outer Worlds.

Dane would have killed himself in that moment, if he could.

But he couldn't even do that. No; he could only hang here in the dimness, paralyzed somewhere between floor and ceiling, waiting...waiting...waiting...

But now light crept through the gloom—a pale, purplish radiance Dane found somehow vaguely familiar.

Then a slight movement of the ship changed his position. His eyes, searching, found the source of light.

It came from the unforked end of the Kalquoi yat-stick Dane had wrapped in plastic to simulate a proton bomb. While he watched, it grew brighter...brighter...as if the metal bar were oozing energy the way a fresh-cut spring twig oozes sap.

Now the radiance grew to an eddying, pulsing ball, so intense it lighted up the entire astrogation chamber.

THE NEXT INSTANT there was a sort of soundless snap. Before Dane's eyes, the radiance transformed itself into a glowing crystal that rose and floated in mid-air.

*A Kalquoi—!*

There seemed to be no pattern nor rhyme nor reason to the alien's actions. Now it hovered; now it darted. One moment it drifted close to the floor; the next, explored the ceiling.

And all the time it radiated changing shapes and colors: a glistening silver corkscrew...the dull grey of a microreel case…pale blue ovals that resembled nothing Dane had ever seen.

Then sound came—the muffled clang of heavy hatch-lids. At once, the Kalquoi moved to the astrogation chamber's door and poised there, apparently waiting.

A moment later the door swung open. Two other aliens joined the first.

The three pulsed and glowed together briefly. Then one detached itself from its fellows and moved in close to Dane.

Immediately, he felt himself permeated by a strange, slightly prickling sensation, as if a slight electric current were being sent through him. Warmth enveloped him. The idea of sleep took on unique appeal.

Now the alien moved towards the door once more; and to Dane's intense surprise, he found himself following, drawn along bodily through the gravitationless ship like a towed target. In a sort of roseate haze—for fear, as of the moment, seemed to have lost its meaning for him—he wondered what would happen when he was transferred to the Kalquoi globe-craft. So far as he knew, the aliens themselves had no necessity for breathing, so the odds were against there being any air supply adequate to enable a human to survive.

But instead of moving him to the globe, the alien took him to the carrier in which he'd escaped from Mars; loaded him into it.

A moment later the second Kalquoi appeared, Nelva in tow. In seconds, she was installed in the carrier alongside Dane. Then, as if by magic, the hatch swung shut, and they were left alone.

Minutes dragged by, a dreary procession.

Then, so abruptly the shock rocked Dane, the paralysis that gripped him vanished. Feeling, the power of movement, flooded back into his body. His brain clicked into high gear, no longer dim nor foggy.

A moment later the carrier's gravity unit came to coughing life. Dane found that once again he had weight and could move about at will.

It brought him a quick surge of relief from inner tension; a sense of control over his situation.

He was glad. He had a feeling he was going to need all such he could get.

Beside him, Nelva Guthrie whispered incredulously, "Clark—! I can move! The brain-drain it's off!"

"Could be," Dane nodded. He felt weak in the knees, just hearing the girl's voice—partly out of relief to know that she'd survived the ordeal of the brain-drain, partly because she seemed to have forgotten or be overlooking their earlier hostilities.

"Then we must be almost to Callisto!" New excitement crept into Nelva's voice. "That's the only way to explain it, Clark. We must be so far beyond the blockade stations that their relays are too weak to maintain catatonia!"

"Maybe."

"Maybe? What kind of talk is that?" Nelva's tone suddenly was tinged with irritation. "Can you offer any better explanation?"

"Yes, I think I can," Dam: answered thoughtfully. "Especially if you stop to consider that the Kalquoi took over back while the brain-drain still had us stiff as boards."

"Still stiff—?" Nelva broke off sharply. Her lips trembled as she drew a quick, shallow breath. "Clark, you can't mean it!"

In spite of their plight, Dane couldn't help but smile wryly. "I can't mean what?"

"You know!" The girl's ash blonde hair rippled as if a chill were passing through her. "You can't mean—that—the Kalquoi—"

"—that the Kalquoi have come up with an answer to the brain-drain?" Dane finished to her. "As a matter of fact, that's just exactly what I think. The way it looks to me, they've licked the thing, a hundred per cent."

Nelva's face was white, her breathing too fast. "But Clark—"

"What's going to happen, you mean?" Dane shook his head. "I don't know, any more than you do. But one thing's certain: if I'm right, as of this moment all Thorburg Jessup's Security blockade stations on the inner-planet side of the Asteroid Belt are just so much scrap equipment."

The girl stared at him. He couldn't read the things in her grey eyes, and when her lips moved the words came out an incoherent whisper. She covered her face with her hands. Her shoulders shook with soundless; racking sobs.

A WAVE OF TENDERNESS swept over Dane, so poignant it made his whole throat ache. Taking the girl in his arms, he held her to him, smoothing the soft hair, bracing her shoulders against the sobs.

The tears stopped, after a moment. Nelva raised her head; looked up at him, trying to smile even while her lips still trembled.

Gently, Dane said, "Don't worry, Nelva. We'll make it somehow."

"Don't lie to me, Clark. I know what's going to happen, and it really doesn't matter." The girl's lips still smiled, but a shadow lay across the grey eyes. "Just one thing, though, Clark: I've got to tell you, and you've got to believe me. I've never betrayed you, not ever, even for a moment." A pause. The grey eyes, falling again. "You see, I've—I've always loved you, ever since the first, so long ago—long before you remember. Only I couldn't help you, didn't dare to tell you, even a little…"

Dane stood very still. "You…didn't dare tell me?"

"No. Because I didn't know enough…about you; your potential…"

"But *what* didn't you dare to tell me?"

Nelva buried her face against his shoulder. Her words came muffled now. "About the things you wanted to know—who you are, where you came from, the hairless man."

Dane's heart pounded. Silently, savagely, he fought against letting his voice soar with his tension; against drawing his arms too tight about the girl's slim shoulders.

"About the silver needle, too?" he pressed gently.

"No. Not that. I never knew too much about the overall picture; only the one part."

The tension was too great. Dane could stand it no longer. Spasmodically, he gripped Nelva's shoulders. "Then tell me what you do know, damn it! Who am I? How did I get on that asteroid? Why weren't my records in your files?"

"Please, Clark!" Nelva twisted. "I'm going to tell you. I want to. There's no need to hurt me—"

"Sorry, Nelva." Dane let go of her; turned away, ashamed. "It drives me, Nelva. I've got to know. Everything, everything…" He drove his clenched fist savagely into the palm of the other hand.

"I understand, Clark." The girl's hand was on his shoulder now. "You see—"

The carrier hit something, with an impact that threw them both, sprawling, to the floor.

Dane braced himself for further shocks. When they didn't come, he scrambled up; helped Nelva to her feet.

Before they could more than right themselves, however, the entrance hatch opened. An unfamiliar atmosphere rushed in, strangely scented yet breathable.

Raw-nerved, Dane stumbled to the open door and looked out.

The carrier lay on solid ground, in the shadow of the great Kalquoi globe-ship. An open port indicated that the smaller craft had been dumped unceremoniously from the larger.

Arm about Nelva, Dane turned now and looked off beyond the Kalquoi vessel.

Then, involuntarily, he stiffened. A chill of excitement ran through him. Instantly—instinctively, almost—he recognized the scene before him; knew the truth.

They stood upon Callisto!

## CHAPTER EIGHT

THIS WAS SANDOZ, man's last stronghold among all the outer satellites and planets…fallen citadel, thirty years abandoned now.

Ruin's hand lay heavy upon it. Crumbling walls and shattered structures sprawled everywhere, and great saw-leaved, turquoise-blue plants half concealed long stretches of the cracked, disintegrating pavement. Scarcely a building stood staunch and whole.

Yet there was no mistaking the place. For though the last edifice might fall, the city's shining silver shaft still thrust up stark and proud into the sky.

Dane stared at it, fascinated, hardly able to tear his eyes away. It was compulsive, the inner drive he felt to draw still closer to it. Yet even though he recognized it as such, he could not fight it down.

Why did it pull him so—this strange, sky-spiking needle? Why, in spite of all logic, did the feeling surge so strong in him that his destiny was bound tight to his half-forgotten hope—gone-dead men called the Sandoz Shaft?

But only one segment of his brain kept up the wondering. For in his heart he knew the answer didn't matter. Not when the tie that linked him. to the needle was strong enough to lure him across a million miles and more of void to certain death, here on this alien fettered world.

Bleakly, he looked across to Nelva, and wished he could be with her in this hour. But the Kalquoi seemed to have rather definite ideas of protocol at this stage, and one of them involved his separation from the girl.

Now, parallel but on opposite sides of what once had been the city's central thoroughfare, Dane and Nelva trudged from the carrier towards the distant shaft. A sort of honor guard of Kalquoi surrounded each of them, directing them in the way they were to go by means of sudden, small, darting beams of light that stung like so many angry insects.

The shaft grew larger as they approached, till Dane was staring up at it in awe. With every step, the compulsive drive he felt to reach the needle grew stronger in him. Nothing else could hold his interest or attention. Once, briefly, he even caught himself wondering why it had seemed so important to him to hear Nelva's answers to his questions; to know his own identity, and that of the fiend-faced man without a name.

As if such could ever matter, when destiny lay at the foot of the Sandoz Shaft!

They reached what must once have been a small park, now. The street they'd followed ended in it. But mere lack of pavement seemed to mean nothing to the Kalquoi. Unhesitating, they herded their charges on across the open green.

And now, on the far side, Dane caught his breath. Before and below him, a broad natural bowl had been developed into an amphitheatre, back in the days of Callisto's human occupation. The metal-rimmed base of the silver shaft stood in the center of the arena at the bottom.

But even the shaft was as nothing in this moment. For never had Dane looked down on a stranger sight.

For Kalquoi crowded the dish-like hollow, hovering like fireflies among the fallen pillars and shrub-masked seats. Hundreds of them; thousands—they pulsed and glowed and changed shape amid the ruins, till the amphitheatre itself was transformed into a fantastic fairyland of energy and light.

But his escorts gave him no time for pause or contemplation. Already they were urging him down the nearest aisle to the arena below.

Then, at last, there was an end to his scrambling and stumbling through the debris. His guards halted him, close by the base of the Sandoz Shaft.

The drive to reach the giant needle boiled in Dane, almost overwhelming. But when he would have tried, a quick flick of light from one of his captors turned him back. He could only stare greedily, drinking in the strangeness of the towering monument with his eyes.

And it was weird enough to hold any man's attention. Just as Dane remembered from his vision, the needle stood unsupported, a silver lance suspended in mid-air, completely clear of base, socket, bedplate.

Studying it here at close range, Dane could see how delicate was its balance. The point quivered visibly where it hung above the socket, dancing like a plastic ball atop an airstream. Vibrations ran the slim length of the needle, till it seemed to turn into a flickering razor-edge of light.

How could it be? A beam of some sort—?

SOMETHING STUNG Dane's flank, then. The pain stabbed so sharp he whirled by reflex, questions and shaft alike momentarily forgotten.

As he did so, a light-beam flicked at his elbow, flame-hot. His guards were urging him to movement again, prodding him diagonally ahead till he stood directly in front of the shaft, but with his back to it.

Now he saw that Nelva Guthrie, too, had reached the arena. Surrounded by her captors, she stood to the left of the shining needle, just as a moment before he himself had stood to its right.

But the Kalquoi gave him little time for such observation. While he watched, a small group of them moved out into the arena and took places in a semicircle close before him.

Dane's guards fell back before the newcomers. In the seating area up along the amphitheatre's sloping sides, the assembled crystalline, light-emitting aliens eddied closer, glowed brighter. A hush seemed to fall over the hollow. Tension climbed like a spaceship at escape velocity.

Dane stood very still. There was nothing he could do but wait.

Then, suddenly, one of the Kalquoi in the tight arc close before him pulsed vivid scarlet. A familiar impulse leaped into Dane's brain...a patterned, rhythmic groping: *John Dane...John Dane...John Dane...*

Dane sighed; tried to concentrate upon his answer: "Not John Dane. Clark Dane. Clark, not John..."

From then on, there was tumult and fumbling and confusion. Wordless and incoherent, alien intelligences probed every fold and convolution of Dane's brain.

Out of it all, for Dane, came not words, but feelings; not intelligibility, but insight. Slowly, deep within him, there began to grow the weird panorama of a race so alien man could never hope fully to understand it. A concept took form—the concept of a life-type composed wholly of radiant energy, without permanent shape or body...beings that found their only reason for existence in the acts of shape-building and light emission. In his mind's eye, Dane saw how they replenished their life-force, transmuting into energy whatever convenient objects came to hand.

And because these aliens, these Kalquoi, themselves had no need for bodies or possessions, they'd been unable to conceive that other species might require such things…might even be harmed if bodies and possessions were transmuted.

But now, at last, glimmerings of this truth had reached them. They'd begun to see the harm they'd done; were sorry for it.

Would man, in his turn, meet them halfway? If they'd stay clear of him and his possessions and allow him to return to the outer planets, would he abandon the disconcerting brain-drain that prevented their shape-changing and transmuting? True, the magnetic shield they'd developed protected them from it, after a fashion. But it was a nuisance. If possible they'd prefer to operate without it…

Numbly, Dane tried to force his aching brain to function. If only he could find the concepts—!

He verbalized it, spoke aloud in hope that meaning would somehow come through: "Yes, yes. Man wants peace as you do. He'll go halfway and more—"

The arc of Kalquoi pulsed approval. All but one.

The others' glow slowly faded.

Instantly, like a bomb bursting, the lone dissenter flared emerald and purple, a radiance so brilliant that Dane reeled back, near blinded.

His brain reeled, too. For such was the burst of energy the Kalquoi spewed into it that flame seemed to sear at every cell. Dane screamed aloud, writhing in torment.

The flame snuffed out. The pain ebbed slowly. But a message stayed, fire-written: *If all men want peace as you say, why have the others scorned us? Why are you the only one to open your brain to us?*

Dane groped. "The others—? What others?"

But no coherent answer reached him; only a jumble of fragments and half-impressions. He sensed that the Kalquoi were arguing among themselves while he stood by, forgotten.

As if to prove him correct, his guards now goaded him back to his earlier post to the right of the Sandoz Shaft. Simultaneously, the other group of guards moved Nelva forward to the spot in front of the shining needle where Dane himself had stood.

Swaying a little from the aftermath of pain and mind-fatigue, Dane tried to watch her.

But now, all at once, his compulsion to reach the shaft was again upon him. It was stronger, this time: stronger than ever before. It was all Dane could do to resist it.

Yet resist it he must, for his captors still stood close by, and he had no taste for the sting of the light-beams they flung at him.


GRIMLY, HE concentrated on Nelva Guthrie, trying to force himself to think of her instead of the sky-thrust lance so close beside him.

Strain-lines marred the girl's blonde beauty now. Her hair was tangled, her cheeks pale, her lips trembling.

And yet, for all of that, she was still the loveliest thing Clark Dane had ever seen. The yearning for her gnawed at him like a physical hunger.

Now the interplay of form and color from the line of Kalquoi indicated they were probing her mind. Dane could see her straighten, just a little...breathe a fraction faster. Her hands moved, rubbing at the side-melds of her garment as if to scrub sweat from her palms.

More shapes, more, colors from the Kalquoi. More signs of tension from Nelva Guthrie. Dane could catch only fragments of the projected thoughts and feelings.

Yet something was wrong. Instinctively, he sensed it. A knot drew tight, deep in his belly. He breathed harder.

To what purpose? No matter what happened, there was nothing he could do. He knew that.

Only—Nelva—

He never finished the thought. For abruptly, without warning, the same Kalquoi who minutes before had sent the searing charge through Dane's dazed brain blazed again—a great flash, orange and white and turquoise. The thought smashed in, so violent that even at this distance—even though it was directed at Nelva—the impact made Dane's head reel: *She-creature, you close your brain to us! You hold back like the others! You want no peace—*

Nelva's scream came like an agonized, overriding echo. Blindly, she staggered forward, clutching her head between her hands.

But the Kalquoi gave no heed. As if the girl were not there, he deluged the whole area with a raging, searing, tidal wave of energy.

Nelva sagged to her knees. Her cry was the keening of a soul in torment.

It was a trigger to turn a man to utter madness. Spasmodically, Dane started forward.

But there was no way to reach the girl, and in his heart he knew it. Too many Kalquoi, too many light-beams, stood ranged between him and her.

But the shining needle, the Sandoz Shaft—it was relatively unprotected for the moment—

Spinning, Dane dived towards it—low, beneath the level at which his captors hovered.

His shoulder crashed against the heavy, buttressed base. His hands closed on a corroded telonium bar. Tearing it from the litter, he surged up, heedless to the light-beams that stung at his back and sides.

The bar had weight to it. Dane swung it with all his might, straight at the seemingly empty space between socket and needle-tip.

If only he could upset the delicate balance of forces that held the shaft upright, and bring it crashing down, almost anything might happen!

The blow hit square and true. But to Dane, it was as if he'd struck the bar against a daggad column. Pain shot up his arms, clear to the shoulders. The telonium strip tore from his hands and sailed through the air nearly fifty feet.

Before the bar even hit the ground, a bolt of energy struck Dane. Helpless, hopeless, sobbing with fury at his own inadequacy, he found himself slammed back bodily against the metal rim that girded the shaft's base. His hands clamped to the alloy.

It was a moment completely incredible; a moment beyond all possibility of belief. For as Dane's hands touched the rim, sparks leaped from flesh to metal. His whole body convulsed. Blue flame crackled in a tight sheath round him. Power pulsed through every bone and muscle in a surging tide.

Then sound came—a high, thin skirl, louder and louder, till Dane thought his eardrums must surely burst.

But the sound still welled and swelled and echoed; and now numbly, it dawned on Dane that something was happening to the Kalquoi. Even blurred as his eyes were, and in spite of the spasms of his body, he could see that one and all, the aliens had reverted to crystal form. No light gleamed in them. They moved jerkily, as if having trouble even rising from the ground.

The sound in Dane's ears reached a new high note—a note so clear and pure it ceased to be sound at all, to human ears. In its place came silence—a taut, thin-strung, nerve-fraying silence that somehow was almost more than flesh and blood could bear.

Now, while Dane watched in the eerie silence, a Kalquoi crystal suddenly cracked wide open in mid-air.

Its shards cracked, too; and its shards' shards. It was dust before it hit the ground.

On all sides, it was the same. Everywhere in the amphitheatre the aliens were shattering to atoms. In seconds, not one of them remained.

Convulsively, Dane twisted; managed to throw one anguished glance upward to the silver needle that was the Sandoz Shaft.

But so fast was the shaft vibrating that it now looked less like a needle than a flash of silver light.

Dane sagged back. Dully he wondered how long it would take a man to die this way. Certainly there must be a limit to the amount of such maltreatment the human form could stand.

Yet he knew strength was not in him to break loose, tear away.

Was this, then, his destiny? Must he die here, a living conduit for the power now activating the Sandoz Shaft?

What a goal for a compulsion! What an end to a dream! He couldn't even see the spot where Nelva Guthrie lay…

Time blurred, after that. There were moments when he was conscious; more when he was not.

When he first heard the drone of the carrier's landing beam, he thought he was delirious.

Then he opened his eyes, and the craft hung there before him, less than fifty feet away. While he watched, it ramped down. The hatch opened.

It was then he *knew* he was delirious, for sure.

Because the first of the two men who climbed out was thick-bodied, bullet-headed, lump-faced, scowling Pfaff, the Security rep with whom he'd clashed.

And the gaunt figure behind Pfaff was that of the hollow-cheeked, hollow-eyed, hairless man, master of slaves, whom Dane knew only as the Being-Without-A-Name!

## CHAPTER NINE

"WELL, DANE, how does it feel to be the savior of your race?"

Slowly, painfully, Dane forced his eyes to focus and search for the speaker.

It turned out to be the hairless man. He sat on a crumbling stone bench, hunched forward slightly and with his teeth bared in a cold, knife-edged smile. Glowering Pfaff stood to his right, scrubbing a palm over a hairy forearm. To his left, a uniformed, strangely blank-faced stranger stood too stiffly at attention.

Dane moved his head a fraction, seeking Nelva.

She sat off away from the three men, still farther left. Her face wore a stiff, strained look, and she kept her eyes on a spot distant from the group, as if to avoid involvement with them.

Dane shifted his gaze back to the hairless man. He still said nothing.

"I do make a striking picture, don't I, Dane?" the other observed as if answering a question. His smile twisted mirthlessly. "If you'd like to try the effect yourself, a proper dose of some types of radiation poisoning will do it. In my own case, the hair follicles were killed completely—scalp, eyebrows, facial and body hair, everything. I felt rather bad about it at first, for I was vain enough in my younger days. But then I found that even the loveliest of women is more apt to be impressed by the unique, the different, than run-of-sex handsomeness; and no man ever forgets me. So there are adequate compensations. Personally, I'm quite satisfied."

The voice held the same twist as the smile—a twist of bitterness, of irony, of lurking menace. It was the voice of a man who enjoyed playing cat-and-mouse or forcing those in his power to confess their thralldom.

The very sound of it made Dane's hackles rise, in spite of all he'd been through. "Who are you?" he asked tightly.

"That's right; you don't know, do you?" The man leaned back a fraction. The lids of the deep-set eyes flickered. "We might make a sort of game of it, even—let you guess—"

"He's Thorburg Jessup." This, quite unexpectedly, from Nelva. Hate rasped in her words. Her eyes were smoldering.

"Thorburg Jessup—!" Involuntarily, Dane's eyes widened. He pulled himself round; sat up.

"Oh! You're feeling better!" Jessup chuckled. "That pleases me. It would have been a pity to lose you, after all the effort I put into your creation."

Dane breathed in sharply. Then, catching himself, he counted off three deeper breaths before speaking: "And...what did you have to do with my creation?"

The Security chief lifted a long fingered hand. "It was my idea. All of it, from the beginning."

"Your...idea—?"

"Precisely. My biochemical staff in the Mercury laboratories is superlative technically, but they need a broader, more incisive mind to shape their concepts. I gave them that—outlined the exact requirements they'd have to meet in developing the type of creature we'd need to send against the Kalquoi."

"The type of *creature?*"

"Of course. You didn't think you were human, surely?"

Dane's throat drew so tight he couldn't answer. Numbly, he dug his fingers into the dirt of the arena, trying to hide their trembling.

Jessup watched him for a moment, then threw back his head and laughed—jubilant, sadistic; the self-same laugh Dane had heard that other time, so many worlds away.

Only then, suddenly, Nelva Guthrie was on her feet—fists clenched, eyes blazing. "Stop it, you fiend!" she screamed. "Stop it! Stop it!"

Jessup's laugh cut off as if severed by a knife. "Oh, my dear! Have I disturbed you?" Mock solicitude flowed from him like oily vapor. "Really, I *did* have to handle it this way, though. I simply couldn't use a human. There was the matter of subconscious memory, inadvertent knowledge. You have to consider those things when you're dealing with telepaths like the Kalquoi, you know."

Beside the Security chief, pig-eyed, smirking Pfaff moved smoothly into the conversation: "You didn't have much time, either, Mr. Jessup."

"A vital factor," the hairless man nodded. And then, to Dane again: "As you may have guessed, the Kalquoi already had perfected a shield against the brain-drain. It was urgent for us to strike a strong blow at them before they seized the initiative. I decided the Sandoz Shaft, here, offered us our best opportunity. We'd already worked out a new-type catalytic relay that would activate it on practically no power. The only problem lay in coupling the relay to the shaft. To do it by normal procedure, with a task force, would have destroyed its whole value because it would have driven the Kalquoi from Callisto."

From Pfaff: "Brilliant analysis, Mr. Jessup!"

"So, I conceived the idea of an artificial man with the relay built in, made part of his tissue structure—a creature something on the order of my guard, here"—a gesture to the blank-faced man in uniform—"but of a higher order. He'd be physically strong, well endowed with initiative. His mind would be good, too, and properly pre-stocked with all necessary information, as well as conditioned to a compulsive drive to reach Callisto and the Sandoz Shaft."

DANE SHUDDERED. Were these the things that dreams were made of—conditioning, packaged data, concepts born in someone else's brain? Was he really one with the blank-faced guard—"but of a higher order"?

He wished he'd died at the shaft's base.

Jessup was still talking: "…and as a special twist, we named you Clark Dane, after a John Dane who stayed on at Sandoz, long after everyone else had left, trying to learn more about Kalquoi culture. Because he'd established some slight communication with them, I thought his name might help you…"

Another piece of the puzzle, clicking into place. Another of Dane's questions answered.

"…like every life-form, the Kalquoi needs periods of quiescence. The yat-stick provides a closed circuit where a Kalquoi can rest with no escape of energy. So, you were left by a yat-stick experts assured me contained a Kalquoi in repose. I knew your name would arouse the creature's interest. Tie that to your drive to reach Callisto, and the odds were good you'd live to activate the shaft. If you didn't"—a shrug—"it didn't matter too much, because you lacked any knowledge detrimental to us."

Of a sudden, Dane was tired of words and explanations. He no longer cared about questions or their answers. Lurching to his feet he stumbled past the Security check, out of the arena.

Jessup eyed him curiously. "Where are you going?"

Dane continued his unsteady march. He didn't bother to answer.

Thick-bodied Pfaff moved round to block him. "Hey, you! Mr. Jessup asked you a question!"

Dane veered to pass him.

Belligerent, bullet-head down, Pfaff thrust a foot between Dane's. Dane tripped and fell.

Now Nelva Guthrie was running to him; kneeling beside him. Her fingers were cool upon his face. "Let him alone, can't you?" she cried fiercely. "Haven't you done enough to him, without more of this torture?"

Jessup's smile faded just a little. "You've been a favorite of mine a long time, Nelva," he said in a too quiet voice. "Don't jeopardize that status now."

The girl stared up at him, face tear-streaked. "Do you think I care about status at a time like this?"

"A dangerous question, my dear." The Security chief studied her for a long, long moment. "Now I find myself wondering if I can trust you further—and no matter how I phrase it, the answer comes back, 'No.'"

Dane felt Nelva's fingers stiffen on his cheek. A tremor ran through her.

Abruptly, his desire to leave the arena ebbed. He sat up. "What happens when you get no for an answer, Jessup?"

"*Mister* Jessup, you chitza!"

Pfaff snarled. But the hairless man himself only smiled faintly.

"A wise man knows when not to talk, Dane," he observed. "For you, this is one of those times. You've done well. I like you. So human or not, I'll look after you so long as you behave."

"And Nelva?"

"She's no concern of yours, Dane. And as I said once, a wise man knows when not to talk." A pause. "I may not repeat that again."

And from Nelva: "Please, Clark. Let it go."

Dane eyed her soberly. "Why?"

The panic flaring in her eyes was more than enough answer.

To no one in particular Dane said, "Everything that can happen to me has already happened. That gives me leeway to take care of a few things."

He started to rise.

Jessup's twisted smile was gone now. All gone. Sharp and hard, he rapped, "Get him, Pfaff!"

The squat Security rep whipped out a pelgun.

Dane went flat on the ground in the same instant. Clawing out, he caught Pfaff's ankle and jerked the leg from under the thick body.

Pfaff crashed to the ground. Twisting, he fired a pellet.

It went wild. Before the Security rep could trigger off a second shot, Dane swung up a ten-pound chunk of broken masonry in both hands and brained him with it.

Jessup's voice echoed, shouting to the guard. The man-creature raced towards Dane and Nelva.

WRENCHING THE PELGUN from Pfaff's dead hand, Dane shot for his new attacker's knees.

The guard spilled headlong; lay moaning.

Pelgun at the ready, Dane swung to Jessup.

But the Security chief's voice stayed calm, even though his hairless skull was glistening. "You can't shoot, Dane. You can't." And then, forceful and vibrant: "Remember? I'm your master. You're my slave!"

Dane stopped in his tracks.

Deftly, while Dane stood as if paralyzed, Jessup took the pelgun. "You see, I'm still master, Dane. I created you. That's why you're going to stay here. You and Nelva Guthrie. Together. Dead."

Sweat came to Dane's forehead. In an agony of desperate tension, he tried to drag up his hand.

But it was like being thrown back through time into a nightmare. Once again, it was as on that other, dark-remembered day. The control, the conditioning—they gripped him in spite of all his efforts; bound him tight.

"Can you guess why you two will die, Dane?" Jessup taunted. "Is there any reason you can see?"

Mumbling, Dane said, "Because…we know…too much?"

"That's right. But what about?"

"About the Kalquoi wanting peace? About the way you sent me to activate the shaft, so they'd think men were all against them?"

"Very good, Dane. Now tell me why."

"Because you…run things…so long as there's trouble…with the Kalquoi. But if peace comes…you'll be just another man."

"Correct." Jessup's hairless face set in a death's-head grin. "And now, to get on to the business at hand…"

He moved towards Nelva. Face chalky with fear, she stumbled backward, behind Dane, out of his view.

Again Dane strained. Again he failed.

Was it true, then? Was he really Jessup's slave?

Numb, aching, he prayed for some power to break the deep conditioned trance into which Jessup's cue-words had thrown him.

Behind him, then, Jessup said something too low to catch. A blow thudded.

Like an echo, Nelva screamed.

Dane never knew what happened in that moment.

Yet within him, it was as if some tight-confining band had snapped. The new stimulus overrode the old. Whirling, leaping over Nelva's crumpled form, Dane threw himself bodily at Jessup.

The Security chief's voice, half-choked, gasping the cue-words: "Dane! Remember! I'm your mas—"

The voice cut off as Dane wrenched the hairless head back and jammed a hand down the yawning throat.

Jessup, arms flailing. Jessup, eyes bulging. Jessup, face purpling.

A final jerk, with every ounce of strength left in Dane's sagging muscles. The *crack* of bone snapping.

Jessup limp. Jessup dead.

Dane knelt beside Nelva. Hands shaking, he felt for her pulse.

Her eyes opened; grew tender. Slowly, she smiled. Her slim hand clasped his big one.

A shudder ran through him. Face averted, he pulled his hand from hers and drew back.

"Clark—!" She caught at his elbow. "Dane, it's all right. I'm not hurt, not badly…"

Wordless; again he tried to pull away.

Nelva came close now; clung to him. "Clark, what is it? What's wrong? What have I done?"

Dane choked. "It's not you. It's me; what I am."

"What you are—?" She tugged him around and stared at him, grey eyes ever so wide. "What are you, Clark?"

"You hard Jessup say it: I'm…not human." Miserably, Dane forced himself to meet her gaze. "Don't you understand, Nelva? I don't even dare to think about—you and me. I'm—different. Like no one, not even Jessup's Zombie guards."

A moment of silence. A long, echoing moment, while the girl sat with eyes downcast.

Then, slowly, she looked up at Dane once more. "I know, Clark. Better than you. Because I've had longer to be lonely."

"To be lonely——?"

"Yes, Clark." Nelva's grey eyes suddenly were tear-filled, her voice a whisper. "You see, I was the first—the very first the lab made with a real mind, and free will. That was why I had to find you, even though I didn't dare tell you anything for fear I'd distort your reaction pattern, put you in danger." A smile, slow and shy, tremulous through the tears. "That's over now, Clark. We...don't have to be lonely any more..."

The pickup ship came much too soon.


# THE END

*If you've enjoyed this book, you will not want to miss these terrific titles…*

## ARMCHAIR SCI-FI & HORROR DOUBLE NOVELS, $12.95 each

**D-91**   **THE TIME TRAP** by Henry Kuttner
**THE LUNAR LICHEN** by Hal Clement

**D-92**   **SARGASSO OF LOST STARSHIPS** by Poul Anderson
**THE ICE QUEEN** by Don Wilcox

**D-93**   **THE PRINCE OF SPACE** by Jack Williamson
**POWER** by Harl Vincent

**D-94**   **PLANET OF NO RETURN** by Howard Browne
**THE ANNIHILATOR COMES** by Ed Earl Repp

**D-95**   **THE SINISTER INVASION** by Edmond Hamilton
**OPERATION TERROR** by Murray Leinster

**D-96**   **TRANSIENT** by Ward Moore
**THE WORLD-MOVER** by George O. Smith

**D-97**   **FORTY DAYS HAS SEPTEMBER** by Milton Lesser
**THE DEVIL'S PLANET** by David Wright O'Brien

**D-98**   **THE CYBERENE** by Rog Phillips
**BADGE OF INFAMY** by Lester del Rey

**D-99**   **THE JUSTICE OF MARTIN BRAND** by Raymond A. Palmer
**BRING BACK MY BRAIN** by Dwight V. Swain

**D-100**   **WIDE-OPEN PLANET** by L. Sprague de Camp
**AND THEN THE TOWN TOOK OFF** by Richard Wilson

## ARMCHAIR SCIENCE FICTION CLASSICS, $12.95 each

**C-31**   **THE GOLDEN GUARDSMEN**
by S. J. Byrne

**C-32**   **ONE AGAINST THE MOON**
by Donald A. Wollheim

**C-33**   **HIDDEN CITY**
by Chester S. Geier

## ARMCHAIR SCIENCE FICTION & HORROR GEMS SERIES, $12.95 each

**G-9**   **SCIENCE FICTION GEMS, Vol. Five**
Clifford D. Simak and others

**G-10**   **HORROR GEMS, Vol. Five**
E. Hoffman Price and others

www.ingramcontent.com/pod-product-compliance
Lightning Source LLC
Chambersburg PA
CBHW030309180626
46810CB00003B/987